THE DESPICABLE FANTASIES OF
QUENTIN SERGENOV

written by
Preston Fassel

Cover Art by Dan Gremminger

Encyclopocalypse Publications
www.encyclopocalypse.com

For my parents, who have always accepted me as I am, and who still love me even though I write stuff like this.

Without obsession, life is nothing.
-John Waters

ONE

2002

Static images flicker across Quentin Sergenov's television screen, black and white speckled ghosts of his glory days in the squared circle. He watches from his bed, supine; lime green, golf-ball sized eyes stare wanly from their recessed sockets. The lights are off in his bedroom, as they have often remained since the day he first moved in to the warehouse he now calls home. This is not the result of narcissism or shame; Quentin has come to enjoy his appearance, even take pride it in— particularly the iridescence of his purple and turquoise plumage— and the occasion is not rare that he will find himself preening before the mirror in a manner not dissimilar to when he would comb his mustache and coif his once voluminous hair, admiring its sheen and the squareness of his jaw, the simultaneous coldness and warmth of his steel grey eyes. His *new* eyes, though— the green ones—suffer from extreme photosensitivity. During his rare excursions beyond the confines of the warehouse, he has discovered that a pair of sunglasses which attach to the face via an elastic cord provide sufficient comfort. Wearing them for prolonged periods, however, is irritating, so he chooses to keep the lights shut off unless absolutely necessary. He can see quite well in the dark, in any case.

Apparently, the Deinonychus was a nocturnal creature.

A wave of static sweeps the television screen and the already fragmented images of the men onscreen distorts even more, their compact, muscular bodies now only appearing as abstract dots periodically dancing across the screen. Tears roll down the sides of Quentin's elongated face; he discovered soon after the surgery that he is still able to cry, and made a notation in his journals that the Deinonychus apparently possessed tear ducts not unlike those found in humans. Quentin raises a long, clawed finger to his face and wipes away the tears; the loss of his wrestling programs is almost more than he can stand. He has been losing the picture on his television periodically over the past few days, but cannot figure out why. His satellite provider tells him there is nothing wrong with the signal. He believes them.

Quentin reaches across the bed and picks up the remote, raising the volume on the television set. He finds that by hiking it up to maximum, he can still make out the color commentary quite clearly, and this brings him some pleasure. Even if he does not have the picture, he can still hear the grunts of the men as their arms entangle one another, and the hollow thump as their bodies strike the mat, the vain shrieks of their ringside managers and the sarcastic innuendos of the commentators. There was a time when Quentin, too, was one of the Adonises, shorter than most at five foot eleven, but more technically capable than many of the other wrestlers in the Backbreaker Championship Wrestling Federation. Quentin had come to the federation following a life of much hardship: born addicted to heroin in a North England brothel, courtesy of his mother's own abuse of the drug—whether she had ever died from it was a matter of minor but ultimately inconsequential research in Quentin's adult years— he spent the first several months of existence clinging to life. He was at last released from the hospital just in time to enjoy his first birthday as the guest of a foster father he only ever knew as Mr. Tibbins, an amiable old librarian who bore a gross resemblance to Fred Rogers in appearance and dress, but not in the manner in which he began beating Quentin shortly after the boy's coming out at fifteen. A subsequent year of regular belt-whippings presaged his eventual flight to the United States on board a fishing trawler whose crew he briefly joined in exchange for passage, instilling in him both a solid work ethic and a galvanized determination to prove himself above Mr. Tibbins' base humiliations and insults. Too, his time at sea sleeping in the same clothes day-in, day-out prepared him for the many years he spent similarly dozing in the back of a decade-old Impala on an aimless tour of the United States, building his professional wrestling experience and reputation on the farm circuit via appearances at the country's innumerable bingo halls, VFWs, and local arenas, supplementing himself with a variety of odd jobs of the legal and extra-legal variety while racking up an impressive laundry list of concussions, broken bones, and unfortune- though thankfully non-fatal- venereal diseases.

Most men would have used termed these circumstances "traumatic;" Quentin prefers to term them "inconvenient."

In spite of his hardships, he had achieved his greatest ambition, albeit late in life; he was the oldest man in the federation upon his debut, a staggering thirty-nine, the age at which many other wrestlers begin to feel the ache of bone chips and the painful culmination of too many injuries gone untreated. Still, following an impressive display of technical showmanship at a well-publicized regional event featuring some of the BCWF's old performers coming out of retirement for the night, Quentin had managed to catch the eye of Frank Bauman, the owner of the federation, who saw in him great potential for a marketing gimmick: a man twice the age of his roster of superstars who could still match any of them in stamina or endurance, and with the readily publicized visage of someone a good decade younger, scars be damned. That had been '93, and the other major federations were slowly siphoning BCWF's business with better production values, more marketable talent, deeper pockets, and fewer steroid trials. Frank needed a win where he could get one; he had signed an eager Quentin to a small but lucrative contract that very night.

It was neither the first nor last time Quentin would be exploited by the empty promises of someone he trusted.

Quentin rolls off the bed, pausing to take a fond look at his wall mural of Molly Ringwold, Jon Cryer, and Andrew McCarthy posing for a *Pretty in Pink* promotional still, painted for him by a dedicated local artist who asked few questions and who was only too happy to accept a well-paying gig from a patron she never had to deal with except over the phone. Moving past the mural he goes to an ornate walnut bookshelf where he keeps the collection of old issues of BCWF's official *Backbreaker Digest* he has been steadily accumulating on eBay. The magazines have been selected with great care; he does not purchase them in lots, nor does he indiscriminately buy every issue he comes across. He bases his selections solely upon his knowledge of their photo spreads; he is particularly fond of the issues which feature full-color centerfolds of his favorite two performers, Griever and Wave.

Quentin removes a penlight from the bookshelf and uses it to begin perusing his magazines until he finds the issue he is looking for. It is the November 1992 issue, featuring a centerfold of a then-twenty-six-year-old Daniel Phillips, still performing under his birth name, prior to his 1995 assumption of the role of a charismatic, laid-back, surfboarding fan-favorite cast in the mold of a beach party hero named "Wave" to capitalize on the 60s nostalgia craze. In the photo, Wave is the perfect picture of male beauty, washboard abs poking out over generic red spandex trunks. Wave's hair is cut into a flowing, silky black mullet, the color of which perfectly matches his carefully trimmed goatee and eyebrows.

Quentin knows from experience that Wave is a natural blonde.

Quentin long ago learned to take advantage of his new attributes. The length of his maw allows him to comfortably hold the penlight while utilizing his arms for other tasks, though he must take care not to clamp down too harshly. The first time he attempted to hold a Maglite between his teeth he bit too hard on climax and accidentally chewed it in half, battery acid spilling back into his mouth and searing the enamel off of many of his eighty teeth.

Quentin's eyes lock onto the image of Wave: hands on hips, massive pectorals soaked in sweat, a single drop of moisture dangling from the tip of his left nipple. Quentin feels the moisture on his own face again and lifts his sunglasses to wipe it away; he makes sure not to allow his claw too near to his eyeball, to avoid scratching the cornea.

Quentin is careful not to allow his torrential saliva to spill across the picture of Wave, an act which would surely ruin the centerfold. While the average human mouth produces roughly one liter of saliva per day, Quentin generates double this amount every hour. Although he must take care to keep his mouth closed when near leather or most cottons, the tiled floor is easily cleaned with the bleach and ammonia which he has delivered to him weekly along with his regular supply of filet mignon, caviar, vodka, and Pinot Noir. During his brief time at the top Quentin Sergenov had saved well, and as such was able to accumulate a small fortune in his days as BCWF performer; while still affording himself small luxuries he had never given himself over to the profligacy that claimed the bank accounts of so many of his younger coworkers, and his prudence has more than justified itself. He keeps the money in an interest building account, which will allow him to live out the remainder of his days in his current lifestyle. How long, exactly, that shall be, barring illness or accident, is a matter which Quentin tries not to focus on much; there is no existing scientific data on the lifespan of the Deinonychus.

Quentin cleans up his mess and then washes his hands thoroughly. His warehouse is minimally decorated, which keeps it easy to clean. He takes special care to ensure that all surfaces remain free of dust and dirt and that his dishes are washed meticulously. All of this is done not out of any fear of germs or contamination, or even any particular loathing of dirt or disorder; rather, it is done for the protection of his editing equipment, so delicate and sensitive that even the tiniest speck of dust might compromise its mechanical integrity.

Quentin moves to the editing room and observes his Movieola, to ensure that it has not been disturbed by any arachnid or insect. The room is lit with a single red bulb. Quentin inspects the machinery with a glint in his eyes not unlike the one that resided there while he surveyed at his magazines. This look, however, is more extreme; its' intensity far surpasses the human concepts of either love or lust.

<u>TWO</u>

1995

Suddenly, Wave couldn't remember how he'd gotten into the ring.

The arena lights were especially bright that evening, and the roar of the crowd more deafening than usual; his world became a blur, a spinning cornucopia of odious colors and deafening sound. He wrapped his arms around Quentin to deliver a German suplex and he could smell Quentin's sweat, heavy and musky. It sent a warmth through his body from the nostrils to the groin, not unlike taking a mouthful of wasabi. Quentin's body seemed tougher this evening, his flesh tighter and more youthful, his muscles more defined. Wave shook his head and focused on the performance; it wasn't the first time this had happened to him. He was on the road over two-hundred-fifty days a year, and in the middle of his third marriage, to a woman he was sure was cheating on him. The thought filled him with rage, even though there was a part of him that knew he couldn't blame her. Even when he was home, they rarely made love; his body was too beaten and bruised from his nights in the ring, his body too sore, his limbs too weak. After weeks of being slammed against taut canvas, thrown in the air, having his head banged into steel chairs and two-by-fours, there was little energy left for copulation, as hungry as the flesh might be. The realization had dawned on Wave in the third year of his career that, essentially, the only physical contact he experienced anymore was with men: sweating, oiled-up men in prime condition. Friendly, companionable, *beautiful* men. With this realization had come fleeting images; and as those images began to linger longer within his mind, they soon turned to considerations.

Not that he had ever acted on them.

General BCWF wisdom held that of course *some* men might get an idea or two in their heads every once in a while; that was life on the road, spent nominally in the company of other men in prime physical condition, with no guarantee of affection from either amorous valets or that stripe of particularly eager groupies known as "ring rats"— more frequent in legend and locker room gossip than in the field—said to lie in wait outside post-show locker rooms, eager to leap on the first superstar they saw. No, those ideas were to remain strictly that, though- passing, unwelcome, invasive flights of terrible fancy never to be realized. To have done would mean being forever branded as one of those few, despicable *things* weak enough in character to have submitted to their basest urges. No performer would ever enter into the ring with them again; and then the poor soul would be a pariah within the entire organization, ultimately leading to the dreaded "queer blacklist." Such men were forced to retire in shame and humiliation; perhaps, if one was lucky, he might find work in the backwater world of so-called "underground wrestling," that nightmare realm that existed beneath the amateur circuit in obscurity and barbarity, performing one or two shows a week at truck stops and Mafia-run strip clubs for crowds of inbred hicks and convicted sex offenders in attendance in the hopes that they might see an accidental death or severe mutilation.

This was not a fate that Wave wished for himself.

As was scripted, after the German suplex, Wave

followed up with a swinging neckbreaker and then his finisher, a modified powerbomb called the Luau; Quentin was pinned, the ref counted to three, and Wave was declared the victor. He retreated quickly to the locker room, to separate himself as soon as possible from the physical presence of Quentin Sergenov. He scurried to the shower, tearing the laces from the eyelets of his boots, stripping free of his tights and hurling himself headlong into the shower. His hand fumbled for the knob and he turned it on full blast, letting out a scream of shock as the icy water beat against him. The urges began to retreat.

He would remain strong.

"Good show you put on tonight."

Wave spun around. There was Quentin, stripped bare, walking towards him. Quentin stepped to the shower pole directly beside Wave's and turned it on; steam began to build up at once from the heat.

"Thanks." It was customary for wrestlers to converse in the shower; the talk was friendly, casual. Family, friends, gossip about other performers and plans for the evening's dinner were common shower room topics.

"I think we really got the fans worked up with that new finish. We're building heat. Frank might be moving us to main event status soon if we keep it up." Aside from the obvious prestige factor, main event status for wrestlers in the BCWF was particularly sought after for the pay increase it carried with each performance.

"Hey." Quentin moved closer to Wave and stuck his hand beneath the water, withdrawing it quickly. "That's freezing, man. You sick?"

Quentin reached across and turned the hot water faucet on Wave's shower. Wave's body went rigid as the heat began to wash over him.

"You're tense. You were pretty tense in the ring tonight, too." Quentin placed his hand on Wave's shoulder. Wave was about to move away when the realization dawned on him that it was not a conciliatory gesture; Quentin's fingers tightened around his flesh and moved down to his bicep. "You need to relax."

Quentin and Wave looked each other in the eye, recognized the mutual desire, the mutual need. They gripped at each other's faces; the hair of Quentin's mustache and Wave's goatee entangled as their lips collided in a frenzy. Wave flung himself against the wall, palms flat, offering himself up. Quentin hurriedly moved to the locker room door, shutting and bolting it before returning to the shower, slipping on the wet tile and falling against Wave's back. He braced himself against Wave's hips and then took his prize.

THREE

2002

Memories of that first time still bring about feelings of bittersweet reminiscence in Quentin. He dreams of it often; it is usually what is on his mind when he sits at his editing equipment, long, lithe claws working with nightmare dexterity. The Deinonychus was an extremely agile creature in every aspect of its physicality, from its toes to its eyelids. The claws and legs are responsible for the most awe-inspiring feats. The claws—there are three of them on each hand— are an average of four inches long and as thick as hot dogs. They taper towards the end like sickles; the tips are capable of slicing human flesh with precision comparable to that of a freshly stropped straight razor. Quentin's legs are masses of compact muscle, and can easily break down a dead bolted door with a single kick. He can jump six feet vertically with ease; through experimentation, he has learned that the five-inch long, scythe-shaped claws on each of his feet, when propelled in an arc by the force of his legs, can enter a frozen side of beef without much effort. Quentin has only once ever used this capability on human beings, and the results were such that police officers responding to the scene were said- according to subsequent message board gossip- to have required extensive counseling for posttraumatic stress disorder. Quentin does not like to dwell on this, especially while working on his video editing; they are unpleasant thoughts about days he wishes to leave long behind him. He prefers to focus on happy memories: his first encounter with Wave; their subsequent encounters, hushed rendezvous arranged in whispers during matches, stolen moments in quaint roadside diners where the failing light only added to the atmosphere of forbidden romance.

Quentin leans back on his tail, a stiff, bony apparatus which eliminates the need for a chair. He has just finished editing his latest art film. It is his own customized copy of *All Hands on Dick*, a war picture. It is the romantic and heartwarming yet action packed tale of a young ensign named Rex Steele who enlists in the U.S. Navy just days prior to the start of the Vietnam War. In between firefights with the Vietcong, Ensign Steele learns what it means to be a man, courtesy of his bunkmate, a Vietcong prisoner of war, two Army surgeons, and, in an intensely romantic climax, his commanding officer. Utilizing a VHS of a BCWF pay-per-view and his video-editing equipment, Quentin has spliced in clips from BCWF matches; sometimes in lieu of the connecting sequences, sometimes just snippets in the midst of them. The editing is crude; during the love scenes, the static faces of Wave and Griever periodically appear over those of Ensign Steele and his costars, their mouths hanging open even as characters speak.

Spliced into the love scenes, in segments of twenty-four frames at a time, are portions of *Pretty in Pink* and *Jurassic Park*.

Quentin plays the final scene of the movie and watches, satisfied with a job well done. It is, perhaps, his finest achievement; he hopes, one day, to possibly submit one of his videos to an art gallery for exhibition. Until then, they provide him with a constructive hobby, one he has been able to monetize through a small but relatively lucrative web business called "Bill's Thrills," using the alias Bill Baseman to sell his tapes to interested connoisseurs and collectors. Though he is financially secure Quentin likes to think of the profits from his tapes as validation of his skills. Occasionally, he receives fan mail; Quentin always provides polite replies, though he declines in-depth discussions of his artistic vision. Besides concerns for his anonymity, Quentin prefers his audiences to come up with their own interpretations of his work.

Quentin reaches into his desk and removes a cigarette; because of his anatomy, he requires a foot-long holder in order to properly partake of the vice. Quentin lights his cigarette and places the holder between his thin lips, inhaling and closing his eyes as he listens to beautiful music that only he can hear. Quentin is careful to blow the smoke away from his video equipment; he is fully aware of the ramifications of the smoke compromising the equipment, but it is an addiction from which he cannot free himself, and the satisfaction it gives him as he watches his work is incomparable.

After the song in his head is finished, Quentin switches off the film and goes back to lie in bed. The picture on his television has returned, but his wrestling program has ended and the station has begun airing an infomercial for male enhancement supplements that will last for the duration of the night. Quentin lies on his back and closes his eyes, listening to the soothing voices of the retired porn-star hosts giddily offering their insomniac customers a brighter middle-age and restoration of their lost youth and vigor. His breathing quickens as he begins to fall asleep; he hopes he will dream of Griever and Wave, their bodies entwined and joined in a mound of flesh that has no beginning or end. Should he not dream this, though, it will be of no great disappointment, for he knows that within a matter of time he shall make it a reality.

FOUR

1995

"This is wrong."

Quentin and Wave laid beside one another in Quentin's room at the Marriot. Quentin was prostate, relaxed, every muscle in his body limp; Wave, however, lay fetal, his lower lip halfway into his mouth, teeth digging into the top of his chin.

"What're you talking about?" Quentin turned, ashes from the cigarette clenched between his teeth spilling onto the bedspread.

"I'm married, Quint."

"You told me yourself she's probably cheating on you."

"That doesn't make this OK. It's...wrong. It's just...wrong."

Quentin shook his head and put his hand on Wave's back. "Don't let people start making you think that way."

Wave jerked away and sat on the edge of the bed. "No one's making me think anything, dammit! You *did this* to me. I never would've... I never would've fucking done this if you hadn't have fucking made me! You grabbed me in the shower and fucked me up the ass, you fucking *queer*!" Wave stood up and turned to Quentin. "You son of a bitch!"

Quentin smiled softly. When he spoke, his voice remained calm, soothing. "Wave, I understand how you feel. My first lover, I felt the same way. I beat the hell out of him once, as a matter of fact. But you need to let go of that after a while and come to terms with who you are--"

"I'm not a fucking *homo*! I used to be a fucking altar boy!"

"What's gotten into you?" Quentin's eyes registered concern. "We just finished making love."

"Making love? That's what you call this? Making love? You really…" Wave's voice trembled; there was a terrible sound in his head like a piece of glass caught in a garbage disposal, obscuring rational thought; the more he tried to push it away, focus himself, the louder it seemed to become, only enhancing his mounting rage even more. "OK, you want to know what got into me, I was fucking horny, OK? I've been really fucking horny and I just needed to fucking come. And over the past two months you've fucked me all out and now I realize how fucking sick everything that I've done really is. It's like… it's like being in prison!" Wave picked up a lamp from the bedside table and hurled it at the wall. Quentin winced as it exploded into pieces and then buried his face in the sheets he held wadded between his hands.

Wave's face flushed red. The shame of the past two months of his life, the shame of what he was doing now, overcame him. He breathed deep and put his hand on the wall to steady himself.

"I'm not going to say anything about this, Quint. Not to no one. Long as you do the same, we should both be fine. You're a good guy. I don't want you to lose you your job over this. But I can't do it anymore."

Wave collected his things, got dressed, and left. Quentin spent the rest of the night sitting on the edge of his bed, staring out the window onto the sparkling city night, like a jeweled heaven beneath him. When the sun rose, stared at it, too, his eyes red and raw, until the sky began to cloud over and a gentle mist coated the window. Then he stood and strode into the bathroom, found a complimentary shaving razor, cracked it open, and drove the blade sideways across his forehead. At first there was no mark; then a second passed and the lip of the wound frowned wide, a curtain of blood flowing down his face to mask it with a crimson veil.

<u>FIVE</u>

2002

Shortly after his transformation, in a moment of depression brought on by his isolation, Quentin recalled reading how Ted DeVita- the immunocompromised young man immortalized in one of Quentin's favorite films, *The Boy in the Plastic Bubble*- once said that the only place he was never stared or gawked at in his immune system-preserving space suit was at a *Star Trek* convention. Immediately, Quentin had logged onto the internet and discovered that a sci-fi con was to be held nearby the following week. He sneaked over to the convention center two nights before it commenced and was the first person in line; at once he was admired for the skill put into crafting his "costume," the laborious hours it must have taken, the exquisite attention to detail. He was asked to pose for photos. Celebrities permitted him to skip ahead in line for autographs and pictures; Jeff Goldblum waived his normal fees, to Quentin's endless delight. A family from Akron invited him to join them for dinner.

He was accepted.

He was *loved*.

Today Quentin is once again at such an event. He wears a black leather vest to hold his wallet and loose change; it is the same oversized design originally made for the McGuire Brothers, the world's fattest identical twins and motorcycle enthusiasts, and is now offered as a special order through several leather catalogues to which Quentin subscribes. Once more he has been able to effortlessly fit in with the crowd. He is admired; children, mistaking him for one of the dinosaurs from *Jurassic Park*, ask for his autograph. He smiles broadly, signs pictures, poses for photos. When he no longer wishes to be a spectacle and simply wants to soak up the ambiance and enjoy the silent company of others, he seeks out a lecture hall and positions himself in the back to listen to whatever sci-fi icon from days gone by is talking about life after stardom.

The speaker today is named Benny Deutsch, a sixty-year-old man who once had an uncredited role in the original *Star Trek* television series as an ensign killed by a hostile alien in the opening scene of a first season episode. Quentin listens intently as the heavily jowled Deutsch grumbles on about his experience in a thick Cajun accent:

"A lotta people downplayed my character over the years, mostly on account I never got my name in the credits and I didn't have any lines, but I'm glad now that in this age of the internet and more intellectual debate that Ensign DuFrense—that's what I named him, on account there was no name in the script—is gettin' more attention. Lotta people don't realize how important Ensign DuFrense was. It ain't obvious to a lot of folk, but *Star Trek* wasn't made for dummies! You gotta have a head on your shoulders to understand it."

At this point several people in the audience cheer and applaud.

Deutsch continues: "Ensign DuFrense was a young man, fresh out of the Academy. You can tell this in the episode by the way I carry myself—unsure, still wet behind the ears." A video screen beside Deutsch, which until this point has remained blank, lights up as a silent video of his scene in the episode plays.

Deutsch goes on: "See how there's some terror in his eyes, and how he isn't so straight in the back, not as confident as Kirk or the others. Now look at the way Bill—Bill Shatner, Kirk—looks at me here in this shot, he knows that DuFrense is a rookie, he cares about him. You can really sense some concern coming from Kirk here, some avuncular feelings, maybe even some paternal love."

Onscreen, Ensign DuFrense is suddenly struck by an alien death ray. His body freezes and is tinted bright pink before it fades from view. Quentin gasps and holds a claw to his mouth. He recognized the look exchanged between Kirk and DuFrense; he is sure that he knows what relationship there was, what Benny Deutsch is really attempting to tell the audience, but is afraid to verbalize, for fear that even here, amongst the most tolerant members of society, he will find bigotry and ignorance.

"Now this here, you see Kirk scream, look at that rage, that loss. You go back now, you watch *Search for Spock*, when Kirk's boy, David, dies, there's that exact same reaction, see. *Search for Spock*, it reaches all the way back to this one scene in the series, this one seemingly insignificant scene, and it really brings it home. Kirk's grief over David is compounded—compounded cause to him, he losing DuFrense all over again."

Deutsch continues speaking for several minutes; Quentin does not hear it. His eyes and thoughts are focused on the image of Ensign DuFrense as the scene of his death continues to play in a loop. Quentin expected to come to the convention, socialize, and return home.

He never expected to be *understood*.

After Deutsch concludes his lecture, there is a brief Q&A session. Quentin listens intently, hanging on each of Deutsch's words as he answers questions on topics such as the craft services arrangements on *The Original Series*, his opinion on the future of the franchise, whether he feels *Deep Space Nine* should be considered canonical, and whether or not he knows if the convention center offers parking validation. Once the panel has finished and fans began to file out, Quentin waits until the crowd disperses and Deutsch is left with just a pair of loyal devotees. Only then does he approach. As he does, Quentin regards the people beside Deutsch. There is an athletic woman in full Klingon regalia, including a particularly well made ridged head-piece; she wears a steel bodice which does wonders to emphasize her already impressive bust. Not wanting to seem uncouth, Quentin averts his eyes; he focuses his attention instead on the other person left in Deutsch's company, a roughly five-foot-six, three-hundred pound, tow-headed boy with extreme acne, a doughy complexion, and thick, round, tortoiseshell glasses. The boy wears a red command uniform as featured on *The Next Generation.* Quentin smiles at the boy. The boy smiles back and waves nonchalantly, giving the impression of someone perhaps no longer certain of the borders between reality and fantasy.

"Mr. Deutsch, sir?"

Deutsch's eyes widen as he sees Quentin. "Well, ho there! You from Jim Henson or Stan Winston?"

"Neither, sir. It's a homemade costume."

"Well fuck me runnin' boy, you really know your shit, don'tcha? That there is one professional lookin' getup you got on."

"Thank you, sir. I almost feel ashamed being here like this today. After that speech, I think you deserve all the attention."

Deutsch guffaws heartily, the flesh of his jowls vibrating in rhythm with his laughter. "Y'all right, boy. What's the name?"

"Quentin Sergenov."

"You a Russkie?"

Quentin bristles slightly but feels he can't entirely judge a man probably reared on years of British Soviets in Hollywood war films; he is, after all, a fan of them himself. "My ancestors were, sir. I, myself, am a Yorkshireman."

"British fella, huh? That's all right. Well Quentin, you already acquainted with me, and these here fine kids are fans just like yourself, Betty and Gary."

"Hi," Gary says, raising his hand up again. His voice is adenoidal, his sinuses so obscured with allergenic phlegm that it sounds like '*Hoy.*' After he speaks, he produces an asthma inhaler and takes a puff.

"Betty here is on spring break, and Gary… Well, Gary's classmates sent him here all the way from Vermont."

Quentin cocks his head, curious. "And why's that?"

"Some guys on campus videotaped themselves throwing me into the gym shower in my uniform," Gary says, sheepishly. His face, already almost pink from the pizza-like smattering of acne that covers it, turns bright red. "They put it online. You've probably seen it."

"Not at all," Quentin says. "I'm not into *cruel* humor." He places a hand on Gary's shoulder consolingly.

"He was so brave," Betty says, her eyes trailing up Gary's corpulent form with visible lust. "He barely cried, and he kept fighting all the way until he blacked out."

"Gary here stopped goin' to college for a while, 'til some fellow Trekkies found out 'bout his plight and helped start a charity drive to reward him for his suffering. His classmates all pitched in and sent him here."

"Mr. Deutsch helped!" Gary says excitedly. "He had me custom fitted for this new uniform and he's paying for my hotel room."

Quentin turns back to Deutsch. "Is he now? *Well.* What you said, sir, your insight into Kirk's relationship with the ensign… Startling. You've opened my eyes."

"Always pleased," Deutsch says, proudly.

"There's a thousand guest roles on the shows and, you know, most of 'em have stories, they just never get developed or recognized. Every character in the universe has a story behind them. None of em are there as filler. Not a one."

"I like the Klingons," Betty says. "I once had an audition to play a Duras Sisters crew member in 'Redemption: Part Two,' but my car broke down. I hitchhiked to the studio but the guy who picked me up wanted to stop for lotto tickets because he said it must be his lucky day, and by the time he got his $100 and dropped me off they'd already cast someone. Isn't that just, like, totally *sad*?" Her voice is husky and breathless and she recounts the story- her eyes locked intently on Gary's, though the fogging of his glasses largely obscures them- with such mounting excitement that by the time she reaches the final word she's worked herself into nearly orgasmic thrall. Gary's face reddens in response, nearly matching the color of his uniform.

"The *Star Trek* universe lost what would probably have been its brightest star," Quentin says. "Then again, who am I to judge? Obviously, my interests lie much more in the vein of…*dinosaurs*. I rather… *hate* that word, actually. It feels… *degrading*. Too much of a dark history associated with it. 'Look at the dinosaurs, daddy,' like some sort of sideshow attraction. Someone really ought to come up with… Oh, never mind. Mr. Deutsch, sir, I know you must get this all the time, and I really—Oh, listen to me, like a schoolboy!—Do you have any time? Perhaps to pick your brain, maybe get a bite to eat? I'm sure you must be famished."

"Well that sounds pretty good, but it'd be awfully selfish of me. Betty here's been waiting all day to talk to me, and I helped arrange for Gary to come here myself. I was his friends' contact at the convention."

"I'd be more than happy to bring them along. My only condition is that we either use a car that's big enough to fit my costume or we walk. It's quite difficult to take off, and as I'm sure you can all understand, I'm much too attached to it to just leave it lying around where anyone can steal it."

"There's a Mickey's across the street!" Gary says excitedly. Quentin can see the gleam in his eyes at the suggestion of free food. The boy takes another puff on his inhaler, the excitement putting strain on his already belabored lungs.

When they make it to Mickey's Burger Barn, Gary, Deutsch, and Betty order their food, for which Quentin gladly pays, though he does not order anything for himself. He claims that he has already eaten, but in reality considers fast food a commodity beneath a man of his wealth and taste, and so sits content to speak with Gary, Betty, and Deutsch as they partake of their grease-laden swill.

"This is the best day of my life," Gary says, nearly in tears, in between massive bites of the three triple cheeseburgers he's ordered.

"Slow down there, son," Quentin says, "You're going to choke. Mr. Deutsch, would you say that Captain Kirk had any other…similar…relationships with other ensigns?"

"Well, as a scholar of the show, I'd have to say no. Kirk's relationship with DuFrense was…special."

Quentin nods. "That is magnificent. I always knew that there was a side to Kirk that the audience never got to see, beyond the whoremongering and bravado… I knew that it was all just a ruse."

"Of course," Betty says. "He was probably one of the most complex characters ever written for television…*After Picard*."

"*After* Picard!" Gary chimes in.

"I, myself, prefer Sisko," Quentin says, "Though after today's revelations, I find myself with a newfound admiration for our dear James Tiberius." Quentin's thoughts drift idly to visions of a young Kirk leading Ensign DuFrense into his quarters. He wonders if perhaps Kirk was able to begin the poor boy's education in manhood before his tragic demise. In his mind's eye, the face of Captain Kirk subtly begins to shift until he assumes Quentin's human face, though it is covered in feathers, a melding of his old and new identities. Ensign DuFrense's face first shifts into that of Ensign Steele, before transforming into Wave. Quentin shakes his head and returns to the land of reality, quickly shifting his thoughts to the over-salted French fries spread out on the table before him.

"I always wished they'd made Scotty a captain," Betty says, undressing Gary with her eyes. "I think big men are sexy." Betty leers at the boy over her double milkshake. "Like, I've always found that big guys tend to be the *most... passionate...* they just rarely let it show."

Quentin attempts to diffuse what is becoming an increasingly uncomfortable situation for himself. "What about you, Gary? Where do your interests lie? Say, which aliens do you like best? You a Klingon boy or more of a Romulan sort of guy?"

"I dunno," Gary says. "All of them, I guess. Isn't that what *Star Trek*'s about, everyone getting along?"

"*Quite*," Quentin says. After a moment he clears his throat. "You know, I have, back at my place, the complete *Original Series* on remastered DVD, and a high definition television. I think we ought to go back there and watch our friend Mr. Deutsch's moment of glory in *all* of its glory."

"Oh, cool," Gary says, his eyes lighting up. "I wanted the DVDs for Christmas last year, but my mom got me a sweater instead."

Quentin sighs. "We never get what we really want, do we?"

<u>SIX</u>

1996

"Just dinner. Please."

"No, Quint."

Wave slammed the door of his locker and picked up a bottle of water, pouring it over his head, an old wrestler's trick performed just prior to stepping into the ring, to give the illusion of intense sweat. He fixed his tights in the mirror and began the journey out towards the ring.

"Come on. What's the harm in dinner? Just... dinner."

"It won't be just dinner, and you know that."

"It will. *I swear.* Can't we just be *friends?*"

Wave froze. The sincerity in Quentin's voice chilled him to the bone. When Wave spoke again, it was with the calculated consideration of what roads might lie ahead of him depending on his decision: "No. You're a good guy, Quint. A good athlete. I respect you. So I don't want to see you lose your job. But if you keep this up, I'm going to Frank."

Wave turned and walked silently towards the ring; halfway to his destination cameramen fell into place, and Wave instinctually struck up the posture of his character, crotch thrust out, shoulders back, hands on his hips. Quentin watched him disappear in front of the curtain separating the arena aisle from the backstage, listened to the roaring cheer of Wave's thousands of fans. He was a face, a favorite; his laconic delivery of promotional spots and easygoing demeanor endeared him to a generation of young men who saw in him the living embodiment of their own dreams of an eternal, weed-fueled beach party. Quentin himself had been a face upon his arrival, too, playing the role of a down-on-his-luck middle-aged man who finally realized his dream after a lifetime of hardships and a trip across the ocean to the U-S-of-A, the immigration angle- he'd come from one of the *good* countries, after all- endearing him to the BCWF's base of diehard patriots. It was, of course, the story of Quentin's own life, which added to his fan appeal, and shortly after his debut he gave a series of unscripted interviews over the course of several weeks in which he detailed his life's failures and dreams.

Within a few years, though, the gimmick— like Quentin, whose stamina and endurance began to betray him due to the twin stressors of nightly shows and his own advancing age— grew tired. It was a novelty to see an old man fighting; when the novelty wore out, though, and the old man was still fighting, the fans began to see him not as inspiring but as pathetic. As merchandise sales dried up and people began to boo at the sound of his entrance music—*Man in Motion*, Quentin's own choice—he'd been made into a heel, a villain, an object of scorn. His character, to his chagrin, never changed. He was still the old man realizing his life's dream, but now, instead of being a figure of inspiration, he was one of ridicule: a pathetic has-been trying to recreate his own youth by cruelly preying on those who actually possessed it. The refined Englishman who loved America became a jingoistic effete whose love of finer things was an affront to the federation's nominally blue-collar fans. Even worse, he had been made into the most pathetic kind of villain there was: a jobber, a professional loser, relegated to being pummeled and humiliated show after show as a means of building the reputations of up-and-coming performers— a professional whipping boy. With Wave's final rejection, Quentin was now forced to analyze himself and wonder if perhaps he had ceased to be Quentin Sergenov the man and instead become Quentin Sergenov the character.

Quentin wandered back into one of the locker rooms. It was deserted. In the center of the room was a weight bench, a kind of backstage staple of the BCWF; the wrestlers Frankie T. and Jackie B.B. had purchased it on a lark at a garage sale in San Francisco a few years prior and now transported it with them wherever the BCWF went. It was for the communal usage of all the wrestlers, both to pump their muscles before a match and as a means to relieve stress. Quentin lay back on the bench and reached his arms up towards the bar; silhouetted against the overhead fluorescent lights, Quentin got the brief impression that he was reaching towards Heaven.

One. Two. Three. Quentin lifted and lowered the bar ten times before at last letting it slam down with a metallic thud of frustration. Lifting the weights was not having the desired effect. Quentin sat up on the bench and put his head in his hands. Something was missing. He needed relief; he needed *release*.

Quentin made a cursory glance out the locker room door to ensure that no one was in the vicinity before he went to his duffel bag and retrieved a glossy sheet of paper folded into quarters. Returning to the weight bench, he pulled up a folding chair and positioned it parallel to his head before unfolding the paper to reveal a twelve inch by fourteen inch poster of Charlie Chaplain, dressed as his Little Tramp character, posing with his hands folded mournfully across the top of his knobby cane. Quentin lay back on the weight bench and began to lift again, this time focusing on the poster. Chaplain's soul was a beautiful soul, misunderstood by his time, as evidenced in his oft neglected but artistically magnificent musical composition *Smile*. Quentin knew that it was this song, rather than Chaplain's comic endeavors (as hilarious as they might be) that encompassed his true being; a genius mind forced to lead the life of a phony, an artist masquerading as a clown, damned by society to hide as something he was not. Quentin felt his heartache; he felt simpatico. They were men alike. Perhaps, if their times were different, they could have been friends.

His eyes locked onto Chaplain's; Quentin could feel their souls meet, across the barriers of life, death, time, and space.

In the most desperate corners of Quentin's tortured mind, he wondered if they might have been more.

Quentin began to grunt as he lifted and lowered the weights. The veins in his arms began to pulse. He abruptly rose from the bench, added another ninety pounds, and resumed lifting. His teeth clenched and his nostrils flared. All at once his tights felt especially confining. Quentin again let the weights rest, this time jerking his tights down to his ankles, wadding them up over his laced boots before lying back again. He pumped faster, harder; Chaplain beckoned to Quentin, the Little Tramp's sad, dark eyes crying out, the baggy clothes tenting his body and hinting at the treasure hidden beneath their rolls and flaps. Quentin slammed the weight bar down, one hand gripping it with a strength bordering on rage, the other--

"*What the fuck?*"

Quentin sat up, nearly banging his head on the weight bar. One hand remained between his legs; Charlie Chaplain stared accusingly from the chair. In the archway was Matthias, the new Amish themed wrestler, twenty-four year-old rookie fresh from the farm league in Georgia.

"Holy fuck," Matthias said. He stepped back. "You're a fucking homo?"

"This isn't what it looks like," Quentin tried to

say, though he was too exhausted to speak audibly.

"You're a fucking homo," Matthias repeated, a declaration this time rather than a question. Quentin shook his head weakly; he had come too far, gone to too great lengths to cover his affair with Wave, to have his secret discovered in such a sloppy and careless and embarrassing manner. He would have preferred to have been glimpsed in a clinch; at least then there was the dignity of another participant to the act. This—alone, on a weight bench, with a wrinkled poster—was just *pathetic*.

"Wait," Quentin whispered. He reached his hand out, beckoning to Matthias, not for affection but for understanding, sympathy.

"Don't fucking talk to me! Don't fucking touch me!" Matthias turned around and stormed away. Quentin at last brought both hands up, and allowed his face to fall into them; then he sobbed quietly and waited for the end.

<u>SEVEN</u>

2002

The four convention goers find their way back to Quentin's warehouse, the walk brisk but taxing for Deutsch and Gary, Quentin lagging behind to keep up with them, though he could have sprinted home and back at least twice in the time it takes them to get there.

"This is your place?" Betty asks with amazement.

"I used to work in pro sports," Quentin says. "It paid very well. Now. Let's keep the lights off." Quentin removes his sunglasses. "The picture looks best in the dark, without the glare of the overhead lights."

Gary, Deutsch, and Betty are suitably impressed with Quentin's television, though it is quickly becoming apparent to Quentin that Betty is more interested in fucking an internet celebrity, no matter how obscure, and that Gary is more interested in performing insidious atrocities upon Betty's cleavage. Quentin considers this for a moment, shuddering, before the thought occurs to him that this might play to his advantage.

"Anyone care for a drink?" he asks, trotting to his meticulously maintained antique liquor cabinet. He opens it and produces a bottle of imported vodka.

"Well fuck me runnin' on a chainsaw," Deutsch says, his jowls pulsating in a manner that Quentin finds strangely erotic. Quentin pours him a tumbler, and then another for Gary, which the boy consumes in a single gulp. When she's served her drink, Betty takes small, birdlike sips which Quentin finds somehow personally offensive.

"And now, the show," Quentin says, tipping the bottle between his lips and allowing a stream to flow down his gullet.

"Wow, you can drink through that thing?" Gary remarks. His voice is heavily slurred; Quentin is surprised that the boy can shotgun a tumbler of straight vodka and not flinch, then be sloppy drunk seconds later.

Quentin inserts his copy of the DVD containing Deutsch's episode into the player. He turns on the television; the show begins. Gary grins wide.

"Oh wow, it's so real!" He slurs with zeal, taking a puff off of his inhaler.

"It's a twenty-four-inch plasma screen," Quentin says with audible pride. "Top of the line. I spared no expense."

When the young Deutsch appears onscreen, everyone cheers; Betty reaches over and grips Gary by his neck rolls and sticks her tongue down his throat. Deutsch is either too inebriated or too enraptured by the visage of his youthful self to notice; Quentin, disgusted, leans across to the couple and whispers:

"I have a guest bedroom in the back."

Gary and Betty rise and make their way towards Quentin's spare bedroom, their hands already yanking at each other's clothes. Deutsch, smiling drunkenly, remains unaware of their absence; when the sounds of Betty's energetic shrieks begin to echo through the warehouse, Quentin turns the volume up on the television and then extends the bottle of vodka towards his guest of honor.

"Care for some more?"

"Don't mind if I do." Deutsch takes the bottle and begins drinking straight from it. He keeps his eyes fixed on the television, a wistful quality coming over his gaze.

"I'm impressed by a man who can hold his liquor," Quentin says. "I've found it's the sign of someone who knows how to enjoy himself."

"Hell, this ain't nothin'," Deutsch says in between pulls on the bottle. Quentin's eyes fixate on the way his mouth molds around the neck, softly sucking at it as he drinks. "When I was that boy back there's age, I was knocking back a fifth of Jack a day."

"Were you now? Do tell. Regale me tales of the young Benny Deutsch. Was he as passionate as our Brave Ensign?"

"Passionate hell, played halfback for Oberlin High in '66, fucked half the cheer squad. Woulda fucked the other half too I hadn't broken my damn ankle. Dropped out a month later, headed out West. Stories I could tell you."

"I'd love to hear them," Quentin whispers, drawing closer, images of a hitchhiking young Deutsch filling his mind; the brave young man against the world, perhaps taking his first ride from a handsome, older, compassionate stranger…

"Just a bunch of bullshit," Deutsch says. Another pull at the bottle; when he's done, he points the neck at the screen. "This here. This is what it's all about. Me on fifty-thousand TV screens in every livin' room in America, or however many they had back then. That was my moment. Day in the sun. You stood in the sun once you ain't never cold again. All you gotta do is remember the heat." A single teardrop trickles down Deutsch's cheek; Quentin feels tears forming in his own eyes as well, wishes that the sentimentality of the moment wasn't being sullied by the ongoing aural assault coming at him from the bedroom, Betty's moans punctuated by the intermittent sounds of light gasps and wheezes from Gary's belabored lungs.

"That's a beautiful sentiment," Quentin says.

"Beautiful my ass, just true is all it is," Deutsch mutters. He fumbles with the DVD remote, tries to rewind the scene; succeeds in accidentally turning the player off. He and Quentin are bathed in soothing blue light. "Get to relive the best day of your life, again and again, and people pay you for it? Aw, that's the dream."

"Isn't it, though? But don't you ever wonder if maybe there are good days ahead?" Quentin leans in towards Deutsch; he can feel the heat coming off of his body, smell the musky odor of sweat accumulating in his innumerable folds. "That maybe your second chance is just around the corner?"

Quentin looks Deutsch in the eye; the man stares back at him blankly. His mouth slowly opens; this is it, Quentin thinks. He purses his lips. This is what he has been waiting for; this is the moment of connection that has eluded him all these years, down all these lonely months; this is the temporal junction point that resets it all, the pain of the past, the uncertainty of the future; the wiping of the slate of all his nostalgic sorrows that gives him that great, looming promised tomorrow he has dreamed of for years. Deutsch's eyes begin to slide shut; Quentin cannot tell if it is anticipation or an alcoholic stupor. He decides that it is the first; closes his own; his black, serpentine tongue slithers out of his own mouth and into Deutch's, meeting his, caressing it, his feathered lips working against Deutsch's in a combination of empathic tenderness and wonton, aching hunger.

"Like, oh my God, *help!*"

And suddenly Quentin is jerking away and Deutsch is muttering in surprise and Betty is in the room, still in her headpiece and upper bodice but nude from the breasts down, her slick, well-toned body glistening with sweat in the blue light of the television. The girl is positively hysterical.

"The fuck?" Deutsch mumbles, his head bobbing back and forth between Quentin and Betty. He and Quentin's eyes meet. There is- Quentin *knows* there is, *thinks* there is- a moment of recognition between the two, acknowledgement of what they've just shared, will share again in a moment- before Deutsch shuffles to his feet.

"The fuck's going on?"

"He's, like, not breathing!" Betty screams this before turning and running back into the bedroom, nearly tripping in the process. Deutsch follows her, his body wading through the air as though it were water, in the manner of a drunk still clear enough in his thoughts to have a purpose of action but not the physical coordination to see it through with any modicum of grace. Quentin is behind them, heart pounding, his own thoughts racing, caught between the ecstatic thrill of the kiss and sheer terror at what awaits him in the bedroom.

The scene: more awful than any he could have imagined, Gary laid out on the bed like a piece of flotsam, his body as white and speckled as the briefs entangled around his ankles. One hand claws feebly at the sheets; the other holds his inhaler to his lips, turning purple beneath the soft overhead lights. He repeatedly depresses the plunger, but Quentin does not hear the tell-tale puff of administered medication; it would seem the boy misgauged how many doses were left.

"Oh my God, like, we were just fucking and then he stopped breathing," Betty says. She looks pitifully to the boy, still depressing the plunger with ever weaking movements of his hand; the vitality is draining from him slowly as his lungs struggle to take in air. Only one part of the boy- one unexpectedly impressive part, Quentin thinks- is still functioning properly, although this seems quite futile under the circumstances.

"Aw right," Deutsch mutters, facing Gary but his eyes lolling in his skull as he attempts to fix on some visual point of reference. "Aw right. Boy Scouts. CPR. Gonna do it. Gonna do this. Boy Scouts. CPR."

Deutsch staggers to the bed, gripping Gary's bulk and rolling him onto the floor. The boy lands on his face with a not inconsiderable thud, Quentin thinking that Deutsch may have allowed him to strike the hard, tiled surface with perhaps too much force.

"Do something, *do something!*" Betty cries. Her pitch is rising, grating to Quentin's ears.

Deutsch rolls Gary onto his back; his nose- among other protuberances- has been crushed by the fall and a thick stream of mauve colored blood begins to ooze down his face and chins. Deutsch recoils from the sight, and in that second the boy's fate seems to have been sealed. He looks up to Betty, hopeful, gleaming eyes lighting up at the same moment a satisfied smirk crosses his face. One hand feebly raises to give her the Vulcan salute; and as she returns it his eyes roll into the back of his head and his overtaxed lungs at last give out.

"*Fuck me!*" Deutsch bellows. Neither he nor Betty notice that- in his slack-jawed terror- Quentin has permitted copious amounts of his saliva to begin pooling around him on the floor.

"What happened?" Betty screams. "Do something!"

"I think he had an asthma attack!" Deutsch says, his voice desperate, his words strained. "Call 911!" The terror having brought some degree of sobriety over him, Deutsch begins to administer CPR.

"What's happening?" Betty cries.

"Call an ambulance!" Deutsch bellows in between puffing air into Gary's already dead lungs.

"Where's the phone?"

"That's not a good idea," Quentin says. Tension tugs at his voice; he had not considered every possible contingency when inviting the trio back to his apartment.

"Call a motherfuckin' ambulance!" Deutsch bellows. "Aw, fuck me." Betty looks to Quentin hopelessly; his mind dissolves into an array of disturbed and disjointed thoughts before descending into a state of blind panic. Instinct—Quentin is unsure whether it is his own, or the long dormant physical direction of the Deinonychus—kicks in. Quentin swings his body around so that his tail strikes Betty in the back of her legs; the force of the blow is enough to pop her kneecaps out, rendering her immobile. In the same motion, Quentin lunges on top of Deutsch, pinning him atop Gary's body. His movement is graceful: With a quick stroke, Quentin drives his claw into the base of Deutsch's neck and quickly jerks upward. When it exits the top of Deutsch's skull, the man's brainstem, left eyeball, and a softball sized chunk of pinkish, foamy matter are attached to it.

Quentin hears soft movement behind him and spins around to see the prone Betty, peering blankly at the ceiling, her mouth hanging open, dazed. Quentin stares into her eyes and sees only the vacant gaze of shock, a look he saw many times in the faces of rookies with whom he grappled in the ring, after they'd been piledriven or suplexed or drop kicked, beautiful, stupid young men realizing too late that they'd gotten in over their heads. There is only the slightest twinkle in the corners of each of Betty's eyes—robin's egg blue, Quentin notices, a shade *not* naturally occurring in Klingons, if his *Star Trek Encyclopedia* is to be trusted, and really, shame on her for missing such an obvious detail in an otherwise flawless costume. He finds his leg quickly slashing outwards to rip Betty's torso to shreds. As he struggles to calm his legs, he scolds himself for being so reckless, so reactionary; he dreads the thorough cleaning which will be required this evening. He hopes that no splatter has managed to reach his editing equipment, that no dust mites inadvertently become coated with the trace elements of blood and drift into its sensitive internal mechanisms.

When Betty has been reduced to a soppy abomination, Quentin turns back to see that a large quantity of Deutsch's blood has already spilt out onto Gary's slowly stiffening body. Quentin raises his claws to his face and begins to cry uncontrollably; the energy which would have been dedicated to trashing his apartment in a fit of rage has already been sapped by his annihilation of Betty and Deutsch.

When Quentin has exhausted all the tears that he has to offer, he slowly rises and moves to Gary and Deutsch. He runs the tips of his claws over them, softly, so as not to carelessly break their flesh. Then he lights up a smoke and turns and moves to the DVD player, gently removing the *Star Trek* DVD and placing it in its case to ensure maximum lifespan and no environmental damage. Then he retrieves his special edition DVD of *Pretty in Pink* from the shelf. He places the disc in the player, lights up a smoke, and activates it. He skips to the first appearance of Molly Ringwold. Her position in the pantheon of 1980s popular culture as an archetype of rejection, fractured beauty, and simmering sexuality has endeared her to Quentin as nothing short of a celluloid goddess. Blood slowly drying on his feathers, a thin cloud of smoke floating above the screen, he watches the film in the hopes that her heart will be won by the eccentric Ducky rather than the snobbish but undeniably beautiful Blaine. Ducky has cared for Andie since her cold bitch of a mother abandoned the family; Blaine is a smug, smart-assed, privileged, Johnny-come-lately. He is entitled. He is undeserving. He was never there for Andie; he didn't see her through her darkest hour; he didn't hold her hair back while she vomited in that arena toilet in St. Louis because the two of them had gone too heavy on the whiskey the night before the big show. *Ducky* should win Andie's love at the prom in the film's big conclusion. *Ducky* should wrap his arms around Andie, kiss her deeply, and tear Blaine to shreds for a tasty meal.

Quentin clasps Deutsch's fleshy thigh between his claws and slowly rotates it clockwise until the limb separates from the body. This will be the three-hundredth-eighty-eighth time since moving into his warehouse that Quentin has watched *Pretty in Pink*—at least, the three-hundredth-eighty-eighth time since he began keeping count. He watches in the hope that he will be able to *will* the ending to change: that, through his sheer determination in the belief of true love, his hope, greater than the hope any man has ever felt, will reach out across the realms of reality and fiction, past and present, and bring the star-crossed lovers together at last.

Quentin raises Deutsch's thigh to his maw and tears a piece of him away. A few stray tears trickle but the sadness behind them is waning. He felt for Deutsch, truly did; and now they will be together forever.

EIGHT

1996

Quentin was waiting but not ready when Frank Bauman's secretary called him into the office.

"Hello, Mr. Bauman. It's a pleasure to see you. It really has been too long."

Frank Bauman did not appear as intimidating as one would expect from a man who commanded a stable of steroid-addled men capable of totaling cars with their bare hands. Only five foot six, he had a small, moon face, most of it concealed beneath the carefully trimmed bush of his wiry gray beard. He usually wore double-breasted suits, usually olive green, always with yellow sateen shirts and matching silk ties. It was a well-known fact amongst his employees that Frank was as much of a steroid user as his men, and that hidden beneath his loosely tailored suits was a terrifying body so populated by muscle that it prohibited natural movement of the limbs and so covered by tattoos that there was barely a sliver of unmarked flesh to be seen.

"Hello Quentin," Frank said. His voice was nasal and he spoke with a soft lisp; Quentin had wondered about Frank in his early days in the federation, though the man's ravenous appetite for female managers, valets, and coeds shattered his hopes of ever fulfilling those fantasies. "How have you been?"

"Pretty good, pretty good," Quentin said.

"That's not what I hear," Frank said.

"Oh?"

"Let's not get cutesy, Quentin. I didn't get rich by dicking around the bush. Now Matthias tells me he caught you jacking it to Charlie Chaplain."

Quentin winced. "Mr. Bauman…"

"Matthias is new and young and probably stupid, but I keep my ears open and there's been no words between the boys about the two of you having any kind of beef. So I've got no reason to think the kid's got a grudge. Does he?"

"No, sir."

"Well, then? What is it, Quentin?"

"Sir, it's… complicated. You see, ever since I was a boy…"

Frank's little moon face registered shock; then, resignation. "Oy gevalt, Quentin. Some of the boys thought you might be *meshugga* but I never expected this."

"Please, Mr. Bauman…"

"Quentin, I don't hear any denials coming out of you. You are, aren't you? You're a fucking faggot."

"That's an ugly word."

Bauman stepped away, turning his back in thought. "I can't have you in the ring anymore," he said.

"Sir…I'm… I'm not a monster. When I'm in the ring, it's strictly professional."

"Look, Quentin, it's not just this. You've been getting sloppy lately. You don't have an ounce of charisma left, and, let's not mince words, you're getting *fat*. You're starting to look like a *farkakte* slug out there. The fans aren't going to accept that. And they really aren't going to accept a fat, sloppy, *fag* slug. They're going to think you're getting off in the ring. Our audience doesn't tune in to see homo porn. Now look, I don't really give a shit about what gets you off. But our fans do. And your fans write my checks. You shoulda stayed in the fucking closet, *Mary*. It's over. You're done here."

Frank guided Quentin towards the office door. His hand was gentle on his back; consoling, even.

"You'll have my full recommendation, wherever the fuck you end up," Frank said.

Then the door was shut and he was gone.

Quentin had wrestled earlier that afternoon, meaning that his farewell BCWF match had been a loss to Cowboy Roy Szdarski in an unimportant midcard bout scheduled primarily to act as filler and to remind the audience that Quentin and Szdarski were both still in the federation's employ, so that fans would still feel compelled to buy their merchandise.

Quentin found the hallway almost bare; most of the federation office staff had already departed for the upcoming Thanksgiving vacation. It was a wonder how fast word spread; in the span of a single day, Quentin's dalliance with the Tramp had become public knowledge. It only took another two days for Quentin to be recalled to BCWF headquarters for his audience with Frank. God knew that within the next six hours the news would break on the internet. Quentin Sergenov terminated for sodomy; homo wrestler outed after molesting coworkers. The fanboys and marks would have a field day. Frank's offer of a recommendation was worthless; Quentin's career died the moment that Matthias stepped into the locker room.

Quentin stared longingly at the portraits and promotional photos of his former coworkers that lined the office hallway. Amongst them was a publicity still of Wave; he stood so that three-quarters of his body pointed towards the camera, head down and turned in profile, his visible eye cast up. He had never been more beautiful, Quentin thought; in a perfect world, he would have leapt out of the frame and lifted Quentin in his arms and the two could have escaped that awful place. They would have gotten into a white limo and driven off into the eternal night.

Quentin stepped out the front doors of the office. It was freezing cold and ice was beginning to rain down. His belongings were still at the hotel. He didn't care. Half-checking to make sure there were no cars coming, he crossed the street and wandered blindly into the storm.

NINE

2002

Quentin paces his apartment excitedly, puffing away at his cigarette holder, trying to speak but his words coming out as gibberish that falls on the deaf ears of Deutsch's reassembled skeleton, which Quentin has given a place of honor in front of his *Pretty in Pink* wall mural.

"Here! *Here!* Coming *here!*"

The cause of Quentin's excitement is a commercial he happened across this morning while channel surfing. It was an advertisement for the BCWF, announcing the dates for their upcoming "Kill Across America" tour. In less than a week, Griever and Wave will competing together in a tag-team event against the Highway Hellraisers at the amphitheater ten miles away from Quentin's warehouse.

"So much work," Quentin says. "So much, so much." He stops in front of Deutsch's skeleton, which he has propped respectfully into a faux-leather desk chair and secured with baling wire. "You're going to get to meet them!" He claps his claws together. "We're all going to be together!" He looks back at the skeleton and sighs ruefully. "Such a shame," he says. "If the world weren't so barbaric…if you hadn't have been made to feel so ashamed…this wouldn't have to be this way. I'm

55

so sorry, Mr. Deutsch. But I'm going to make it up to you. You'll see, Mr. Deutsch. From now on, I'm going to live for the both of us; my life, and the life you should have lived. No fear, Mr. Deutsch. No shame."

Quentin finds his cell phone and activates it, claws trembling. He takes a series of deep breaths to steady his voice, then dials. The operator answers shortly.

"Directory assistance."

"City hall, please."

There is a brief moment of silence as Quentin waits for the operator to find the number. Quentin can hear the energy of the microwaves through the cell phone's ear piece, their soft hum, a muted crackle like that on old record players. He closes his eyes and listens to the waves travel.

"All right, I have the number. I can dial it for you for a charge of one dollar."

"Please do."

There is another moment of silence. The waves continue to travel. Quentin has considered that, after he finishes with his latest art project, he might attempt to move his technological interests to the next level and begin work on a machine which allows anyone, in the comfort of their own home, to actually *see* microwaves and bask in the beautiful light of their many colors.

"City hall."

Quentin clears his throat and assumes his most professional tone of voice. "Yes. I have two questions. First, what is the cost of ordering blueprints of a municipal building? Second, might I have such prints mailed or delivered to my home address?"

"Blueprints are twenty-five dollars, and, ah, yes, they can be mailed, if you purchase them with a credit card. Delivery takes between three to five business days."

"*Wunderbar.* Do you take Amex?"

<u>TEN</u>

1997

Quentin Sergenov sat up slowly. His back ached from a night spent on concrete, his spine and hips and pelvis all feeling as though they'd been crushed beneath a stone slab. Inches away, a mange ridden dog stared at Quentin, head tilted to one side in a look of curious recognition. Quentin reached out a single, gloved hand and scratched the mutt's neck. Small insects skittered out of the dog's hair and into the indentations of Quentin's wool glove, burrowing themselves deep within its layers; Quentin watched them curiously for a moment until they vanished from sight.

"Nothing for you today," Quentin said, and rose from the ground, his bones cracking. It was, judging from the whiteness of the sun, sometime in the mid-morning, not quite noon but well past dawn; he could make it to the soup kitchen in time for lunch, perhaps even brunch.

Money, of course, was no issue to Quentin. He had more than enough for him to retire comfortably. Comfort, though, was not what he wanted. Like the Mormon women of old who shore the locks of their hair in mourning, and the widows of the Old South who clad themselves in black for a year following the death of their spouses, Quentin's exile was a practice in ascetic bereavement. He had been so foolish as to have lost his job, his final connection to the man he loved; he would suffer his loneliness in as much abject misery as possible; until the day of reckoning; until judgment; until atonement. The day when he woke up looking up into Wave's beautiful, tear stained face; when Wave would kneel beside him and tell him that all was forgiven, that he had tracked him down across miles of urban jungle and human decay, that he had come to take him away from this. Then his savings would be waiting for them, handsome interest incurred; the fairy tale would be complete.

Quentin limped to the soup kitchen. He helped himself to a fresh spoonful of chicken noodle and a heel from a freshly delivered loaf of honey wheat. When he ate, he let the soup soak into his moustache, and the bread crumbs become stuck in it, so that later smell the aroma throughout the day as an olfactory guard against the stenches of his natural habitat and nibble on the crumbs as a late-night snack.

The strong smell of the soup sent Quentin's mind back to a little hotel in the German countryside which, for one night, had housed the performers of the BCWF during last year's European tour. Quentin and Wave had dined on fresh soup and bratwurst, and homemade goulash cooked by the kind, small woman who ran the kitchen, who likewise had handmade the apple streusel served to them for dessert. Quentin and Wave had fed one another the soup and the goulash, grinning and holding back laughter with wry, knowing smiles as they each fingered the bratwurst. They'd enjoyed the streusel in bed together while watching some movie with Diane Lane and Helen Hunt, dubbed into German with butchered English subtitles. There had been no sex that night, only the food and the movie and the flannel bed sheets, and the fresh night air clearing out the odor of their sweaty bodies when they opened up the picture window before drifting off into slumber.

Quentin cried silently, reminding himself-- as he did daily-- of what he'd read on the library computer shortly after his descent into self-induced madness. Wave *was* what he claimed not to be, and it had taken the federation's swarthy young newcomer, Griever, to show him that. The story so far, as elucidated by the gossip rags and rumor mills that comprised the so-called smark community, those fans well-educated and versed in the behind-the-scenes going-ons of the federation: Quentin, the vile old creeper who'd outlived his welcome, had finally taken his despicable fantasies a step too far in an act of locker room debauchery too twisted for words, presenting himself in the guise of Charlie Chaplain in a desperate attempt to win the affections of the innocent and kindhearted Wave. Wave—who, though he had offered counsel to Quentin about his proclivities had never reciprocated any affection—again turned down his coworker, precipitating a vicious assault stopped only by the heroic intervention of recent fan favorite Matthias. The incident led to a termination for Quentin and a subsequent blacklisting within the injury. Guilt stricken for his role in the ruination of another man's life, however inadvertent, Wave had tried to slit his wrists in the shower following a Pay-Per-View event in which his distress was visible and his performance sloppy. Arriving in the showers just in time following his own match, Griever tore the razor from Wave's hands. The two talked. Miracle of miracles, Wave's savior was not only sympathetic to his plight but himself a semi-closeted bisexual. A confidence grew into deep friendship and then something more, a relationship to stand the tests of secrecy and clandestine meetings, intolerance, the scrutinizing eye of the media. Wave had divorced under the protective banner of irreconcilable differences. The other wrestlers knew but didn't *know*, and Griever and Wave were man enough to keep it professional, and so things were kept quietly and comfortably under the rug. The fans could gossip, but without confirmation beyond the whispers of the ring crew or anonymous tips from cameramen who claimed to have caught a quick peck on the cheek or too-intimate embrace, gossip was all it remained. Besides, what would it mean for the he-men of the audience if they had, for years, been cheering on a *queer*? What would confirmation of these sensational rumors- just rumors, after all, just *stories*- mean for them to have sat and watched—some of them for most of their red-blooded, thoroughly masculine, American-lives—while half-nude, sweating *gay men* groped and tussled in the ring? It was unthinkable. Quentin Sergenov may have been a vile freak—who ever *really* liked him, anyway?—but *Griever*—young, handsome, charismatic—the new BCWF Intercontinental Champion, one of the most rapidly successful young stars in the industry, he of the fist-pumping heavy metal entrance jam and irresistible, bad-boy frat character who every woman wanted and every man wanted to be? *Impossible*. And whatever people said about Wave, if Griever vouched for him- well, that was good enough for anyone. No one asked; no one told; and peace was kept. A peace that excluded any chance of reconciliation or rehabilitation for Quentin Sergenov.

When Quentin had finished with his meal and calmed himself enough to walk, he strode to the nearest overpass, where he found a congregation of leathery men in wool coats and trucker hats. A man holding the leash of a one-eyed pit bull explained to Quentin that the name of the game was one man held the sign for twenty minutes, then switched off with the next in line. Every hour, two men went on a booze run with the previous hour's collections. Quentin agreed to the terms and took the sign—WAR VETERANS—WOULD WORK IF WE COULD—PLEASE HELP, GOD BLESS— from a man in a ZZ Top t-shirt. When his shift was up he switched off with a man in a blue flannel jacket and a faded John Deere hat; Quentin joined the others around an upturned orange crate covered in playing cards, passing around a bottle of Tequila with microscopic rat shits bobbing along the grime gilded base. As the day wore on, the men barely spoke; their language was one of raised shoulders and shifting eyes, a sign to their fellow bums that while they were willing to help build the pot, there was neither trust nor love present. The only words spoken genially were muted "Thank yous" and "God blesses" to the schmucks who handed over their coins and dollars out of car windows and offered their sincerest hopes that either Jesus or the government would save the day.

Sometime just before the sunset, when all of the men had gotten a good buzz going, Quentin looked up from a period of mentally forming Wave's face out of cracks in the median to see that several of the men were staring at him.

"Them are some fancy boots you've got on," the man in the hat whispered.

"Thank you," Quentin replied. He went back to staring at the pavement.

"Where chance you manage to find a pair of those?" This time it was the man with the pit-bull.

"My old job," Quentin said.

"What was that?" It was John Deere hat again. "Ballerina?"

"I was a professional athlete."

"A professional fuckin' athlete, right here with us, how the fuck you like that?" the man in the t-shirt said. He reached into his jeans and came out with a soiled watch cap, perching it awkwardly on his head. "Well, tell us mister professional athlete, why the fuck you get to have those fancy ass boots while the rest of us here are in fuckin' shoes with the soles comin' out?"

Quentin's eyes scanned the men's feet. They all wore mutilated sneakers with missing tongues and shredded laces.

"I think I better go," Quentin said. He stood up. There was a disturbing lack of human activity area. No cars; no people. Rush hour was over; everyone was safe at home, with their families and loved ones, snuggling on orange vinyl couches beneath ice-cream-colored crochet quilts, watching re-runs of *Gomer Pyle*.

"Sit the fuck down!" The man with the pit bull. Quentin ignored him; he turned and took a step.

"Sic him, Eunice!"

On instinct, Quentin pivoted; assumed the proper stance to perform a cross-body block. He saw a flash of light, the glow of the setting sun reflected in Eunice's single eye as it soared towards him. Then, all at once, there was a sound like none he had ever heard before in his life: tiny hums and echoes, a dissonance that suggested not only the alien but the unholy.

Quentin had no idea where the van had come from; neither, it seemed, did any of the bums. Certainly, Eunice did not, as the front of the vehicle struck the dog's body with enough force to cause it to explode, its flesh and innards dissolving mid-air into a viscous mass of muted grays and browns and reds, arcing through the sky to land brutally on the median a good ten feet away.

Quentin and the bums stared in disbelief, at the suddenness of the van's arrival, at its impeccable timing. It was a vehicle like none of the men had ever seen before; it was white, enormous, with the flat front of a microbus and the modified suspension of a lowrider. The sides and back bore no windows or insignias or identifying marks; where there should have been a license plate there was a blank piece of cardboard attached with duct tape. The windshield was pitch black; the van's engine produced the bizarre noise Quentin had heard seconds before its arrival, and now, as he stood there studying it, he tried to make out the individual sounds, tiny dings and pops and the constant clamor of metal grinding against metal.

"Holy fuck!" The man in the John Deere cap bellowed. It was the only thing anyone said for what seemed to be a good long time. In another situation, Quentin thought, the men would be drawing weapons and attacking whoever it was that had killed their beloved mascot; but the circumstances presented to them were so foreign, and the van so utterly intimidating, that all of them were helplessly frozen in place.

The back of the van opened up. Sterile, white light rushed out, produced by two rows of fluorescent lights bolted to the interior roof. Silhouetted against the light were a trio of men; at first glance, Quentin believed that he was seeing in the triplicate, the result of shock, perhaps, or the inevitable onset of the DTs; but as his eyes focused, he saw that there were in fact three of them, each one identical to the next. All three had blonde flat-top haircuts; all three wore round, gold rimmed eyeglasses; all three were dressed in matching laboratory coats, white trousers, combat boots, and, most strikingly, red Swastika armbands.

The three men nodded to one another and then turned to regard Quentin and the hobos. Two of them reached into their lab coats and unceremoniously produced MP5 submachine guns, dangling from their shoulders by brown suede straps. The rapidity of the gunfire blended smoothly with the sounds produced by the engine. Round after round tore through the hobos, the guns spewing forth hot lead like the streams from a Summer garden hose, hollow point bullets expanding as they passed through their bodies, leaving their backs blown apart into gaping craters of shattered bone and serrated flesh.

The sight of the last of the hobos hitting the concrete, the remnants of his head softly splatting into a glob vaguely resembling cherry cobbler, was enough to spur Quentin to run. He turned away from the van and darted; the muscles in his legs, long dormant, sprang to life, propelling him forward with awesome force. All of his desire to die, all of his lack of will, vanished. At the basest of levels he still missed Wave, still yearned to be with him once more. Now, though, faced with the prospect of death, each cell in his body, each firing synapse in his brain, seemed to be insisting to him, informing him as if with data gleamed from some holy and secret source, that he *could* see Wave again, *would* see Wave again, but in order to do so, he must *live*.

Two pairs of hands fell on Quentin's shoulders; the grip they exerted on him was more powerful than any he'd felt in the BCWF, and at once his feet slipped out from beneath him with surprise and pain. Fingers dug into him, pinched the nerves of his shoulders and neck, crippling him with agony. He collapsed to the ground. The tiny, cold steel prongs of a taser punctured his pants and sent hundreds of thousands of volts of paralyzing electricity coursing through his body. Quentin shrieked and writhed; two of his teeth cracked against the sidewalk. When the flow of electricity finally subsided, then came the blows, repeated, heavy swings from expandable steel batons. His body immobilized by the stun gun, Quentin was unable to fend off his attackers; the batons bruised his ribs, blacked an eye, reduced his septum to pulp. He wondered if perhaps someone had identified him at the soup kitchen, if this was about bragging rights, about a group of men so hateful and loathsome as to want to be able to claim credit for killing a famous queer.

"Enough." The voice was deep, an eloquent bellow, crisp English spoken with an Austrian accent. "Load him into the van."

The blows stopped; a second later, gloved hands were gripping Quentin's body, and he felt himself being lifted, up towards the now black night sky, up towards the stars and the Heavens and all the glorious peace they offered him.

ELEVEN

2002

"Hey, uh, something weird's going on out here."

Lem Brenner, a member of the BCWF ring crew, raises his walkie-talkie from his hip and answers back into it:

"What's that? I don't copy."

The voice of Alan Budge, another ring crew member, replies: "There's some big ass package out here behind the arena. It's addressed to the Federation."

Lem Brenner pauses a moment. He is a high-ranking member of the ring crew, having risen to a kind of foreman position after twelve years with the company. Lean, fit, but going gray and lacking the physical stamina he once possessed, his working knowledge of BCWF equipment and seniority within the company make him an ideal candidate for supervising the construction of the ring and broadcast booth before shows. While Lem has few friends in the BCWF by virtue of his own diffidence and preference for solitude, he is almost universally admired, a fact of which he remains largely unaware. Lem motions to a nearby crew member, informs them that there is something he must address out back, and then dismisses himself from the arena proper.

It is dark outside; the ring is nearly fully built, and soon fans will be allowed into the building to get refreshments, buy merchandise from a variety of BCWF-approved vendor booths, and find their seats. The show will begin in roughly two hours. Lem approaches Alan, who stands in front of a six-foot-tall crate. Alan is significantly shorter than Lem, heavier around the middle, with a ponytail and untrimmed beard. He has been with the federation for three years and regularly engages in the recreational use of cough syrup. Lem does not respect Alan's drug use but does respect his dependability and dedication to remaining sober so long as he is on the clock.

"What in the hell is this?" Lem asks. He begins circling the box. It is massive, and could easily contain several grown men.

"No clue," Alan says. "I just came out here for a smoke and there it was. No fuckin' clue where it came from. Look, here."

Lem approaches Alan and the two men inspect the shipping label. The address is local, but is identified as having come from a sporting goods retailer.

"What do you make of it?" Alan asks.

Lem pauses a moment. "I think I heard Frank say something about wanting new shoulder pads for the Highway Hellraisers."

Alan kicks the box with his boot. "Awfully big for a couple of shoulder pads."

"Yeah, but remember the ones they wore a few years back, had those bigass fuckin' spikes on 'em, could take your eye out? Had to have been foot long."

Alan nods. "Could be them then… Should we open it up?"

Lem shakes his head. "Shit no. Frank'd be pissed as hell, we opened up something addressed to the federation. Let's get it inside."

The two men move to opposite sides of the box and attempt to lift it; they are each startled at its weight.

"Fuck me runnin'," Alan mutters. "No fuckin' way these are shoulder pads."

"Hell, must be new ringposts or... *something...*"
Lem raises his walkie-talkie to his lips and calls for three
of his largest men to meet him behind the arena with a
hand truck. It takes all five men exerting the whole of
their strength to lift the box onto the hand truck; when
they attempt to wheel the object into the arena, they
discover that it takes three of them to push it into the
room doubling as Frank's office. Finding Frank absent,
Lem orders his men to leave the crate, hand truck and
all, for Frank to deal with. The men depart to go get some
beer from the soon to be opened concession stands, a
reward for an arduous and unexpected job well done.

Six minutes after Lem and his men leave Frank's
office, Frank himself enters, reviewing proposals for
next year's line of BCWF merchandising tie-ins. He is
considering giving one of his rookies, Hans Ballbuster,
a *push*, meaning that a significant campaign will begin
to endear Hans to the crowd and build his popularity.
As such, Frank is considering-- in the event that Hans
is well received-- releasing a line of jock straps shaped
like mangled testes, emblazoned with Hans' emblem, a
bleeding "H" gripped by a fist.

Frank is startled by the presence of the crate in
his office and nearly drops his papers. He sets them
down on his desk, his eyes never leaving the box.
Approaching it, he examines the label. Climbing onto a
folding chair to inspect the top of the box, he notes that,
while it is shut tightly, it appears to have been sealed
from the inside.

Against his better judgment, Frank retrieves a
small penknife from his suit pocket and drives it into
the crease at the top of the box. Curiosity taking hold
of him, Frank eagerly opens the box, failing to consider
the precise implications of the parcel having been sealed
from within.

When the top of the box opens, its four sides
collapse; a massive cube of foam shipping pellets, now
unencumbered by the walls of the crate, come pouring

down around Frank to reveal the object they protected: What appears to be a massive, life-like dinosaur statue.

Frank steps down from his chair and eyes the statue. It reminds him of the velociraptors from *Jurassic Park*, albeit with an avian quality that reflects the latest paleontological research, the sort his eight-year-old nephew is endlessly yammering on about: the feathers look as though they have been plucked from a glossy starling, and the eyes—probably some sort of glass, Frank thinks—gaze out at him with an alarming intelligence.

Frank cocks his head. He turns to reach for his walkie talkie; as soon as his back is to the statue, there is a loud, hollow slam from behind him. Frank lets out a sound of surprise and turns back to the statue. It is still, immobile; nothing has changed about its appearance or its stance; but his office door is now not only shut, it is *locked.*

Frank strides past the statue, his heart racing with sudden anxiety; a frightening sensation has overtaken his lower abdomen, like an icy fist clenching his stomach from the inside out. He has inexplicably broken into a cold sweat.

"Open this fucking door!" Frank bellows, slamming his fist into the office door. It is made of red-painted steel, durable enough to withstand being rammed into with a small automobile. "Hey, open this fucking—"

Frank suddenly remembers the walkie-talkie he had been reaching for a moment earlier. He turns back to his desk, his hand extending towards—

Nothing.

Frank pauses. In the interim between turning towards the door and turning back towards his desk, the walkie-talkie has disappeared. Frank clutches at his chest. Suddenly the white-painted cinder block walls seem much more confining than they did a moment ago, the buzz of the gray fluorescent lights much louder. His eyes dart around the room; it does not take long before they fall upon the walkie-talkie, now clutched in one of the claws of the dinosaur statue.

Frank opens his mouth, unsure of what word or sound or noise he wishes to create. Before he can make up his mind, the statue blinks, then opens its' mouth, revealing rows of awesome and terrible teeth encircling the snakelike tongue, which undulates to produce a voice not unlike that of Quentin Sergenov:

"Hello, Frank. *It's been so long.*"

Frank stumbles backwards, his elbows bracing him against his desk as his feet give out beneath him. Quentin steps off the hand truck, the foam peanuts quietly crunching beneath his feet. Frank shakes his head. His elbows give out and he begins to slide to the floor; Quentin catches him and props him back up against the desk.

"You remember my voice, don't you, Mr. Bauman? Sir?" There is no malice in the inquiry; it is an honest question. Frank nods hesitantly.

"It's much too long of a story, how I got here," Quentin says. "Suffice to say, I *am* here. And I need to know—this is very important— 'Cards are subject to change without notice,' after all… Griever and Wave, they're on the schedule, but, are they *here*? *Tonight? Right now?*"

Frank pauses a moment; the thought occurs to him that Quentin only requires him for information, that if he answers truthfully, he will survive. He opens his mouth; his throat has suddenly become incredibly dry. He rasps out: "Yessss."

Quentin nods. "Thank you, Mr. Bauman. For old time's sake."

Through his mounting terror, a single, nebulous, thought overtakes Frank- the revelation that he is in danger, that—regardless of how absurd the circumstances he is facing, he is, indeed, facing them, and that Quentin Sergenov- against his own suppositions very much alive and, against all logical thought, very much now inhabiting the body of some prehistoric creature- probably intends to kill him.

With a wordless, guttural scream, Frank he musters all the strength within himself, the rippling power of all his steroid-gifted musculature, and flexes for all he is worth, beginning a cascade effect that causes his shirt and suit to tear at the seams, rippling biceps and pancake-sized pectorals and batlike lats bursting through the fabric to grant him maximum freedom and prepare himself for the oncoming assault; and now, freed from the encumbrance of his clothing, his tattooed body almost pulsating with adrenaline, Frank unleashes a series of slurs that increase in intensity and volume with each subsequent utterance before he at last pulls back one powerful arm and delivers a blow directly to Quentin's beak.

Every bone in his hand shatters on impact, a low, dull crunch echoing through the room. Quentin looks at him quizzically as he grips his fist, teeth grit in agony, the already prominent veins bulging even more comically in his neck.

"You know," Quentin says calmly, "I was just going to… I don't know, break your legs or something. But after that?"

Gripping him beneath the armpits, Quentin swings Frank into the wall, holding him place with his arms as one of his feet swings up, the great, curved claw catching him between the legs. Frank tries to scream but the agony stops his voice in his throat and all that escapes his mouth is a dull whimper. A torrent of blood bursts forth from his severed pudendal artery. His eyes begin to roll up into his head as he slides down to the floor.

Quentin looks down with what, through Frank's slowly darkening vision, looks like a grin. "I'm sorry, Frank. I'm afraid you no longer have a place with the Federation," he says, "but when you get to Hell, you'll have my full recommendation." And then Quentin opens wide to eliminate any and all evidence that Frank Bauman was ever in his office tonight.

TWELVE

1997

The first thing that occurred to Quentin Sergenov as he regained consciousness was that he was strapped down to a table; the rough sensation of rope, of rigid metal holding him stationary, alerted him to the fact that he was now a prisoner. He opened his eyes slowly, then shut them again immediately, the light impossibly bright, stinging and burning his eyes. He writhed; the pain was unbearable. Every bone in his body ached; his arms, his legs, his tail-

His tail.

Quentin froze. Something had moved, a foreign structure inside of his body, located at his back, above the clenched muscles of his rectum, something long and tough and strong seeming. Tentatively, he began to move again, to flex his muscles; his arms; his legs; and then, with a rush of anxiety and terribly dread, he allowed the object to move again, swaying left to right, up and down, long, curving, like a bony blade. He opened his eyes again, straining against the light, and opened his mouth up to scream, but froze before he could make a sound. His back was not the only part of him that had been altered; there was a startling unfamiliarity in the very act of *being*, of occupying what had been, until he lost consciousness, his own body. What had they done?

They had mutilated him so horribly as to turn his body into living putty; they had stretched his face and the flesh of his back.

They had turned him into a monster.

They. Who were they? He remembered them vaguely. He shut his eyes again, trying to reformulate an image of them in his mind. His heart began to race; for the first time since regaining consciousness he became aware of a faint beeping sound from somewhere else in the room, sounding in time with his heartbeat. The beeping became louder as it quickened, until it had reached a zenith of both pitch and pace. Quentin opened his mouth to scream. The sound that came out startled him, paralyzed him. It was not a scream at all; it was a shriek; the sound of an eagle, a hawk.

A door swung open, footsteps racing into the room, the sound of a half dozen men babbling, shouting all at once in what sounded like German. Quentin felt a small, sharp pain in his side as a needle pierced his flesh; moments later, he felt a wave of calm rush over him, panicked thoughts still racing through his mind but his body no longer responding to them. He weakly opened his eyes, winced. He opened his mouth and found that he was still capable of speech, though his voice was raspier now, albeit still accented: "The light. The light."

"It would appear that he is experiencing photosensitivity," a man with an Austrian accent said.

"This aligns with our hypothesis that the creature was a nocturnal hunter." Another voice; it, too, Austrian.

Quentin felt something being fastened over his face. "Now try and open them," a third voice said. Quentin remembered that the men who had attacked him and killed the bums all looked the same; now it occurred to him that they all sounded the same, too.

Slowly Quentin opened his eyes; the Nazis had affixed a massive pair of wraparound sunglasses to his face, shielding his eyes from the light. He squinted;

74

he could see now that he was lying on his side on a large laboratory table, the edges barely visible from his vantage point. Beyond that, racks of chemicals, test tubes, beakers, Tesla coils; all the nightmares and horrors of a Frankenstein movie laboratory come to life. Even through the green tinting of the sunglasses the room appeared utterly colorless, devoid of life; everything was stark, sanitized, black or stainless steel, nothing implying or demonstrating the smallest fraction of human warmth.

This was not a laboratory.

It was a torture chamber.

"Good evening, Mr. Sergenov," one of the Nazis said, and stepped around in front of Quentin. "Being of a superior intellect, I and my colleagues are unsure of how to adequately communicate with a lower life form. We long ago abandoned the pursuit of interacting with common society. Please forgive me if I speak in terms foreign to you or above your realm of knowledge. My name is Kaltenbrunner. As you are no doubt aware, you no longer occupy your previous, human form. Allow me to elaborate, in terms perhaps more suited to your level of intelligence. My colleagues and I deprived you—albeit temporarily— of life, by way of blunt force trauma and the delivery of significant electrical currents into your nervous system. During this limited period of what you would refer to as 'death,' you experienced the trepanning of your skull and the removal of your brain. Immediately after this your brain was inserted into the trepanned skull of a specimen of Deinonychus."

"*What*?" Quentin rasped, as he began to struggle against his confines. Kaltenbrunner looked at him impassively, cocked an eyebrow, turned to one of the other Nazis. "Ribbentrop, another anesthetic, please. We shall not tolerate either interruptions or profanity."

"What?" Quentin repeated, a shriek this time. Another needle prick; his body lapsed into a state of total inertia, his ears still hearing, his brain still comprehending, his lungs still taking in air, but otherwise paralyzed.

"I continue, with a digression. The particular specimen of Deinonychus into which your brain has been placed was created for the purposes of this experiment through a series of prior sacrileges and other experiments both literal and figurative in their profanation of the holy. Your mind is now probably attempting to comprehend the nature of such experiments. You would be right to disregard this endeavor. My colleagues and I, being the *Übermenschen*, were, ourselves, initially perplexed at how to go about practically committing such atrocities. It is as adequate a metaphor as any to say that we successfully completed a process which you, in your mortal, corporeal confines, could only understand as selling our souls. The end result of this process was the mental and physical state of being that permitted us to manufacture the Deinonychus body." Kaltenbrunner paused, giving the most imperceptible of nods to Quentin before continuing:

"Returning to the original line of narrative. Your brain was inserted into the Deinonychus body, at which point calculated amounts of electricity were directed into your anus and brainstem concurrent with significant dosages of methamphetamines, testosterone, and a variety of other chemicals substances of our own design. You are the fruit of our many labors. A child of our endeavors. Daddy's little blasphemy."

Kaltenbrunner nodded; another Nazi approached Quentin. Another needle. Seconds later Quentin found himself capable of speech again. "What's going on? What is all this bullshit? Let me go, please. I swear to God, I won't tell anyone."

"I am afraid you cannot leave," Kaltenbrunner said. "You are here as a living monument to our achievements, perhaps second only to our internal combustion engine which runs on human blood." A chill shot down Quentin's spine, a darkly comforting indication that he had retained emotional humanity, even if a mirror would confirm that his physical status as a man had been stripped from him. He remembered the sounds of the Nazis' van and felt a sudden wetness creep over him.

Kaltenbrunner continued: "Your presence in our zoo shall be a constant reminder of our defeat of the great enemy *Nature* and our self-enshrinement in the Halls of Valhalla. You shall live out the remainder of your life span under our supervision, an ongoing source of inspiration, confirming our greatness and driving us to continue our quest of perpetual self-gratification. Sauckel, this is your favorite part of the speech, you go on and give it this time."

Another of the Nazis stepped into Quentin's line of sight, struck a dramatic pose, and bellowed: "Welcome to Hell!"

Moments later the Nazis were upon him, releasing him from the confines of the table and fastening him into a series of chains, an iron muzzle, braces around his ankles, his wrists; as the Nazis gathered their collective strength to heave Quentin from the table, he became acquainted with his new body, the wobbliness of his new, thick ankles, the strange balance struck between his upper torso and the counterweight of the massive tail behind him. He was surprised that, unlike an infant, who too is born into a new body and must develop the usage of it, he was quick to adapt to this new form, immobile only for the amount of time it took him to adjust his balance. He tilted his head down, looking through the slits of his muzzle, examining his new body, feeling the urge to weep but holding back. The Nazis began to jam him in the hips and ribs with cattle prods, urging him onward, sending painful bursts of electricity coursing through his nerves; the sensations were remarkable, at once agonizing and exciting, new stimuli to be explored and studied.

Quentin found himself being paraded down a

corridor, long, clinical, just as stark and terrifying as the laboratory. It was lined with glass-fronted cells imbedded in the walls, a series of zoo exhibits of the terrifying and unnatural. Quentin shut his eyes, stumbled, but every time he attempted to look away or shield himself from the abominations surrounding him, there came another electrical burst. The Nazis were watching him, ensuring that he looked, wanting him to look, eager for him to take in the horrors around him: A dwarf wearing a white leotard and a pointed white hat, his flesh dyed blue and his eyes bulging from their sockets. A man whose legs had been sawn off at the knees and replaced by the legs of a goat, a pair of ram's horns surgically embedded into his forehead. The further down the hall that Quentin and the Nazis progressed, the more obscene the abominations became, until at last they reached the final cell, empty, with a gold plaque bolted to the wall beside it reading "DEINONYCHUS MAN."

One of the Nazis typed numbers into a keypad in the wall and the glass rose up. Quentin was given another injection; he collapsed to the ground within a minute, and then the Nazis hauled him into the cell, freeing him of his confines and then stepping back out into the corridor. Quentin twitched on the ground as the glass descended again, trapping him; the Nazis turned their backs on him at once, slowly moving down the hallway, their departure hailed by a chorus of screams of incomprehensible damnation from their prisoners; their victims.

THIRTEEN

2002

Matthias grunts and clenches his fists; veins bulge in his face and his forehead as he attempts to pass the mass of impacted feces that has sat festering in his bowels for the past week and a half. With a great sigh he ceases pushing and collapses backwards on the arena toilet. Sweat rushes down his forehead. Stinging pains fill his abdomen and groin. He needs to speak to his doctor about prescribing painkillers that do not induce constipation.

Matthias rubs his face in his hands. Aside from the bowel problems instigated by his medication, his body is tense with anxiety. Tonight's match will be either a career maker or breaker; though Frank Bauman had rewarded him with a push for his outing of Quentin Sergenov, thus sparing the federation- in Frank's estimate- potential tabloid embarrassment, Matthias had proven himself a thoroughly unengaging performer, artless in his technical execution, too overly reliant on brute strength and lacking in the natural charisma or personality required of a true superstar. Though he had been quick, on prior occasions, to remind Frank of his role in ridding the federation of a liability, that currency had only gone so far in maintaining his midcard status. Even his desperate offer to perform the same service again— volunteering to seduce his fellow performers in an effort to see who may rise to the occasion in a sort of homosexual sting operation—only baffled Frank to the point of incredulity, and elicited from him the admonition to improve his in-ring game or risk a pink slip in his duffel bag.

He does not yet know that Frank Bauman is no longer in any position to fire anyone.

The door to the bathroom opens. "Matthias, ten minutes to showtime, let's move it." It is the voice of Donnie D'Amato, the show manager, whose job it is to ensure that everyone is in place and ready to go at their designated time. Donnie's brother Scott was once Frank Bauman's personal attorney and the legal counsel for the BCWF, before a scandal involving a series of morgue break-ins caused Bauman to seek the services of an attorney with more conventional vices.

"I'll be right there, fucker!" Matthias presses his hands flat against the creamy white walls of the stall, bracing himself as he pushes again. He feels a soft popping in his skull and relents, fearful of an aneurysm. He pauses, pants, tries again. A moment later the bathroom door opens again.

"I said I'll be right there!"

"Matthias?"

Every muscle in Matthias' body goes stiff. It is the voice of Quentin Sergenov.

"...Quentin?"

"Matthias, is that you, old chum?"

"Quentin, what the fuck are you doing here?"

"Tying up some loose ends. How has your career been going?"

"Quentin, does Frank know you're here? He'll fucking kill you, man."

"Not if I already killed him first."

"What?"

"Doing all right in there, Matthias?"

Rage, confusion, frustration and guilt collide to

form Matthias' response. "I'm fucking constipated man, and I gotta hit the ring in like, ten minutes, so I'd really fucking appreciate it if you'd let me try and take care of this. We'll talk after my match, OK?"

"How about I give you a hand, eh?"

Matthias does not have an opportunity to consider the offer. No sooner have the words left Quentin's mouth than the stall door comes crashing down on Matthias, ripped cleanly from its hinges, pinning him down on the toilet seat. From beneath the door, he can hear vaguely avian sounds, terrifying hisses and snaps; reaching up past the door to try and fell whatever it is pinning him down, he feels a sharp pain in his hand and withdraws it to find all of his fingers missing, replaced by bloody stumps. Quentin has lived up to his promise: Terror lubricates Matthias' bowels and they void themselves with a tremendous splash.

Matthias will never see his attacker, never know what hideous transformation his former co-worker underwent. Quentin uses the stall door to keep him pinned down, his legs becoming a whirling dervish of death, thrashing and kicking at Matthias' calves and midsection. Blood and innards splatter in every conceivable direction, gushing out onto the floor and into the bowl. Quentin keeps the stall door pressed down until he feels Matthias go limp. Carefully he pulls the door back and drops it. What remains of Matthias' dead, mutilated body slides off the bowl and collapses to the floor in a mangled heap, twitching in a pile of his own guts.

Quentin gasps, pants. There are tears in his eyes.

"Two down," he rasps, and then steps over Matthias' body, clutching the rim of the toilet bowl and letting loose with a torrent of vomit.

Frank Bauman did not sit well with him.

FOURTEEN

1998

Locked away in the Nazis' zoo, time quickly became meaningless for Quentin. A lack of windows and clocks precluded him from knowing if it was day or night; twenty four hours a day, seven days a week, dull fluorescent lights lit his cell and the corridor outside, filling the air with a mind numbing, monotonous hum, equaled in its aural torment only by the continuous shrieks and cries from the once human creatures locked away in the other cells of the zoo. Quentin learned quickly to keep himself silent; while the other prisoners bided their time with cries and pleas for freedom, Quentin knew from his initial meeting with his captors that such endeavors would only serve to bolster their already hideously engorged egos. These were murderers; he had seen them decimate the hobos with his own eyes, or at least, with what had been his own eyes at the time. Quentin had seen those eyes again, just once, perhaps a month after his initial capture, when the Nazis had come to take him back to the lab. They had opened his cell just enough to roll a gas canister inside, the noxious fumes and blinding particles crippling Quentin enough so that they could slip inside and muzzle him up. The next thing Quentin had known he was back on the same table on which he had been born into his new body, being poked and prodded with all variety of needles and tasers. It was sometime during the sixth hour of the torture session, when the Nazis had at last finally worn themselves down and required a coffee break, that Quentin had seen it on the wall: his old body. Strapped up with ropes, barbed wire, and old belts, it hung there nude and mutilated like a trophy on a hunter's wall. The arms and legs were stretched, spread eagle; the mouth hung open, toothless. The eyelids had been pried open to reveal empty sockets. On a shelf, nearby, in jars of formaldehyde, floated what had once been his organs, his eyes and liver and testicles suspended silently in the foul smelling liquid and neatly labeled in German.

Quentin had come to expect these torture sessions; the days when the Nazis would gas him and haul him from his cell and lash him to the lab table and play with his body for hours on end, ramming cattle prods into every imaginable orifice, feeding him all sorts of concoctions to test his reaction. They recorded every detail; every blink, every gasp for air, was neatly recorded in black and white marble tablets that quickly filled up with calculations on how much electricity the Deinonychus body could endure before unconsciousness set in, how much cocaine injected into the bloodstream it took to wake the creature back up. Eventually, the Nazis' fascination moved from the purely physical into the psychological. Instead of lashing Quentin prone to a lab table they affixed him upright in a sort of chair, pried his eyes open with clamps and subjected him to sessions of viewing footage of the vilest acts ever committed to film. For hours on end his eyes were artificially moistened while he was forced to endure endless loops of monochromatic snuff films and soul-sickening, morbid pornography, the Nazis eager to see if he might reach a mental breaking point when the body lapsed itself into unconsciousness to spare itself any further torment. When he grew weary, amphetamines were flooded into his system in calculated amounts, rousing him to another few hours of attention. Gradually, the routines began to take their toll. Quentin slowly lost the ability to tell the difference between his memories of abuse at the hands of Mister Tibbins and what was happening to him here in the present; he often awoke prepared to wrestle that evening against some old opponent, sometimes drifting off to sleep at night in anticipation of tomorrow's fishing catch. Months of torment steadily drove from Quentin's mind that hope he had felt while fleeing the Nazis the night they captured him, the idea that he had been spared death to see Wave again. He knew now that he had not truly been spared death; death would have been a gift from the Almighty in comparison to his present situation.

It was sometime in the middle of Quentin's ninth month of captivity that the accident happened. He had been dining on a wad of raw hamburger—his usual meal, rolled into his cell in a cellophane package by the Nazis, the same way they rolled in gas grenades to immobilize him—when a trio of Nazis approached his cell. Over the months he had learned to detect minute differences in their appearances and mannerisms in order to distinguish them from one another. He was fairly certain that the man who now approached his cell was the one named Ribbentrop.

"Good evening, Mr. Sergenov," Ribbentrop said. "I hope you are enjoying your meal. I have come to tell you that it will be your last for several days now. Allow me to elaborate. We plan to initially starve you, then, confine you to a chamber with one of our other pets— one whose companionship we have grown tired of. I trust you have seen Legend?" Quentin did not respond; he recognized "Legend" as the name on the plaque outside the cell of the man whose skin had been dyed red and whose legs had been replaced by goat's hooves.

"Legend was a novelty to begin with," Ribbentrop continued, "and now that novelty has worn out. It is the belief of my colleagues and I that he has one final round of entertainment left in him. That is to say, being consumed by you. Well then. We must confiscate what is left of your meal, now. Can't have you filling up too much."

One of the Nazis with Ribbentrop opened the door to Quentin's cell; as always, it was only allowed to rise enough for the gas canister to be rolled inside. The Nazi pulled the plug; rolled the canister. Usually, the gas was already flooding in by the time Quentin could think to act; time and again he had attempted to knock the canister back into the hall, but every time he attempted this, the door had already shut, and the canister bounced back at him. This time, though, something amazing happened: The Nazi missed.

"Mein laben!"

The canister hit the rim of the cell door and rolled back out into the hallway. For once, Quentin was the first to act; he lunged at the door of his cell, gripped it, and with a great shriek lifted up. The door flung open and he was out of it, barreling down the hall, through the gas. He did not breathe, did not open his eyes, until he was at the end of the corridor, and only then did he turn back to see the cloud of gas slowly dissipating to reveal the prone bodies of the Nazis. He waited a moment; allowed the gas to settle; then he slowly trotted back to look at his captors. Around him, his fellow captives either stared in dumbfounded horror, let out apprehensive cries of victory, or—in the case of the nearly sacrificed Legend—wept silently. Ribbentrop was still vaguely conscious, his eyes half open and streaming tears, his limbs twitching. He babbled softly in German.

Quentin had never taken a human life before. Even in the darkest depths of his abuse, when Mr. Tibbins' belt had rained down lash after endless lash upon him, he had wished not a violent resolution to his torment but a peaceful one; he had dreamed of the day that the man would see the error of his ways and cease the beatings and two may come to some understanding.

Yet now, here, in this hellhole, in this body, after all that he endured, it was his first instinct. Quentin raised one of his feet up, retracting and extending his terrible claw. It would be like flicking off a light switch; like shutting a door. After what had been done to him, why not? What reason in Heaven or on Earth was there to spare these men's lives?

Quentin could not think of one.

His foot came down.

He was shocked, for a moment, not by the act he had just committed but by the ease with which his claw severed Ribbentrop's head. He had only meant to slit his throat; instead, he had cleanly decapitated him. The head separated from the body with bombastic force, propelled by Quentin's inadvertent exertion of strength, ricocheting off the wall and rolling down the corridor, trailing blood behind it. Quentin could not help but smile; freed now, uninhibited by narcotics or iron restraints—uninhibited, it seemed to Quentin, by humanity— vengeance could come so easily. This new body was built for it. This new life had been given to him for it. He raised his foot up again and swung it at the necks of the other two Nazis. Quentin grinned; and for the first time in months, he laughed.

FIFTEEN

2002

In the arena showers, Wave suddenly freezes, an awful chill shooting up his spine and entering the base of his skull. Beneath the steaming hot water cascading down onto him, he can feel his flesh begin to crawl and slowly ooze out cold sweat. His instincts tell him that something is terribly amiss. Without hesitation he shuts the water off and enters the locker room. All is calm; his co-workers lace their boots, tug on their leotards, mock battle in preparation for the show. Griever is in a metal folding chair, reading a tabloid magazine, his feet propped up on a gym bench. Wave looks at him blankly; Griever's eyes drift up from the pages of the magazine and meet with Wave's, and he smiles, and Wave smiles back. The thought suddenly occurs to him how lucky he has been to have found Griever; how their time together has made him not just content, but honestly, truly *happy*.

Wave moves to Griever, takes a seat on the bench beside his feet. Griever looks at him again; Wave smiles back.

"Something wrong?"

"No." Wave shakes his head. "I don't think so." He looks at Griever intently; he feels as if he has not seen him for a very long time and that after this moment he will never see him again. He does not notice it when

Lem Brenner enters to announce that the buffet table has been set up by craft services. One by one, Wave and Griever's fellow performers file out of the locker room until only they remain.

"What's wrong?"

"I don't know. Something. I just…don't…feel…right. You ever get one of those feelings? Like all of a sudden, there's just something…wrong? And you just know that no matter what you do, something bad's gonna happen?"

"Man…" Griever shakes his head ruefully, puts down his tabloid magazine. He lays a strong hand on Wave's shoulder, clutches it tightly. "I think you're having an anxiety attack, man. My cousin Shelly, she used to have them, remember? She'd just be sitting, watching TV, all of a sudden she felt like those guys who smacked her up were back for her, thought they were right there in the living room. But there was nothing. She was safe. And you're safe. 'Cause I'm here, and I ain't gonna let jack shit happen to you, man. I love you. You know that."

Wave smiles. Even in its simplicity, Griever's speech has managed to bring a small degree of comfort to him. "I love you too, man."

"Come on, go finish your shower. Look, everyone's gone! Snack cart's up. We don't hurry, they're gonna get all the good stuff, we'll be stuck with the frozen broccoli."

Wave and Griever share a brief kiss before Wave rises and re-enters the shower. He closes his eyes as the hot water begins to beat down on his body. He turns so that his back is to the shower head, lets it massage his spine, drive the feelings of dread and terror from him. He thinks of Griever's face, its deepening lines and heavy brow bringing him comfort. He wonders what Griever will look like as an old man; he looks forward to finding out.

When Wave opens his eyes he is pleased to see

his lover's face is no longer a manifestation of his mind's eye but is staring back at him from only inches away. He reaches out to touch Griever but pulls away when he realizes that the face is staring back at him with bug-eyed terror; the hair on Griever's head has been pulled taut and a razor sharp claw is pressed against his throat. It takes Wave a moment to register that Griever is being held hostage by a giant bird.

No. Not a bird.

A dinosaur.

A *smiling* dinosaur.

"Wave...*run*," Griever rasps.

Wave is paralyzed. He slams backwards against the wall of the shower. The adrenaline rushing through his system at the sight of his one true love at the mercy of a threat he cannot comprehend cripples him, overloading his nervous system. His knees buckle and then give out and he collapses to the floor, staring up fear.

"He was never this weak when he was with me," Quentin snarls in Griever's ear, before thrusting him forward, slamming his head against the shower wall. Griever collapses to the floor beside Wave. The sound of Quentin's voice is just enough to snap Wave back into reality.

"Quint?"

"Hello, lover," Quentin says, and then his foot thrusts forward, snapping Wave's head back against the wall and into unconsciousness.

SIXTEEN

1998

Quentin made not a sound as he crept through the Nazis' facility, testing out his new body, seeing for the first time what it was capable of beyond the confines of his cell. He could even control his breathing, Quentin found, make it loud and threatening or totally inaudible, make his body motionless as he drew in and expelled breath, the air entering and exiting his lungs with such silence that an observer would surely think he was not even breathing at all.

Quentin quickly concluded that the compound had once been an underground parking garage, owing to its myriad ramps and lack of windows; knocking his claws against the walls returned no echoes. The vastness of the place startled him; he entered room after room, corridor after corridor, each one just as stark white and sterile as the last. Even their living quarters were nondescript: A long, narrow hallway full of stainless-steel bunk beds adorned with white sheets and stiff, pale green quilts. It was like a military barracks, Quentin thought, like what he had seen in war movies when he used to sneak into the cine as a child.

Like what he had seen in the faded newsreel footage of Nazi labs.

As Quentin reached the door leading out of the

barracks he heard voices, faint, clipped; the Nazis. He slipped beside the door and listened; the voices were stationary, moving neither towards or away from him. With the utmost care Quentin took the doorknob in his claws and turned it, opening the doorway just enough to allow him to see into the next room. It was a mess hall, laid out identical to the barracks except with cafeteria tables in place of beds. Portraits of Nietsczhe and Alesiter Crowely hung at the far end of the hall beside Nazi banners, softly flapping in the artificial breeze of an air conditioning unit.

"I have noticed that Ribbentrop's nose is approximately two centimeters longer than the rest of our noses," Kaltenbruner said. He was sitting at one of the tables, across from Sauckel and two other Nazis. "I thought that I had corrected this error during his last plastic surgery, but the girth of his proboscis refuses to be tamed."

"His lack of conformity unsettles me," said one of the Nazis at Kaltenbruner's table. "I move that he be banished from the dining hall until another surgery can be performed."

"Agreed," Kaltenbruner said. "I have also noticed that Hess continues to develop auburn roots in spite of gene therapy." Kaltenbruner raised a tablespoon of gruel to his lips and slurped it down. "I fear that he is genetically contaminated."

"We should feed him to Deinonychus Man," Sauckel said. "Make him an appetizer before we give him Legend."

"It shall be considered," Kaltenbruner said. Another slurp of gruel. He sighed, looked at the wall whimsically. "So, what do you think you'll all be doing for Spring break?"

"Cancun," Sauckel said.

"I think I'm going to stay home with mom and do some extra reading," another Nazi said. "I've almost got enough credits to graduate."

"Prodigious," Kaltenbruner said, monotone. "Then what?"

"I think maybe business school."

Quentin considered the conversation a moment. It occurred to him now, for the first time, his hearing unencumbered by the sounds of high voltage or porn jazz, that while Kaltenbruner's voice was gruff and baritone, the rest of the Nazis' voices were soft, smooth; like the freshly-cracked voices of young men at the tail-end of puberty.

Quentin clutched at his own maw; he had been abducted, transformed, tortured and abused by a group of fucking grad students and their fucking *professor*.

A man and his children.

A man and his *child*.

Mr. Tibbins.

For the first time in years, since before he was fired, since before he even joined the BCWF, Quentin suffered a flashback. Suddenly, he was no longer in the Nazi's facility. He was fifteen years old again, sobbing, cowering in the corner, and before him, knuckles bloody, removing his belt, folding it for the whipping to come, stood Mr. Tibbins, who, as Quentin now remembered—*thought* he remembered, *might* have remembered—looked an *awful* lot like Kaltenbruner.

An awful lot like *all* of them.

"Daddy!"

The Nazis turned to see Quentin come barreling into the room, screeching, batlike wings spread, his claws thrashing. The first two he hit were dead before their bodies landed on the floor, their flesh and organs shredded into strips of fleshy ribbon that came raining down on their comrades like bloody confetti at a Fourth of July Parade in Hell. The Nazis screamed; they ran; they fumbled and tripped over one another.

Quentin was sobbing now, bawling as he tore them apart. Not one of them were spared. Viscera soared through the air in balletic arcs before landing in gelatinous piles on the floor, steaming in the frigidity of the artificially cooled air; arterial blood exploded across the walls in great, deep crimson streaks that trailed fine rivulets to the floor. Quentin leapt about the room, soared over the heads of his prey as they ran for this door and that, came down on their shoulders and snapped their spines just as they thought they had escaped the fate of their fellow classmates. He devoured the chunks of flesh and bits of organs he caught between his teeth as he snapped and chewed at them, until there was only Kaltenbruner left, immobilized but alive, the impact of Quentin's landing on him having shattered his pelvis and luxated his eyeball, which bobbed from his dangling optic nerves as he feebly tried to crawl to safety.

"*You,*" Quentin bawled, his face now red with gore. "I trusted you, daddy."

"*Gott in Himmel!*" Kaltenbruner shrieked. Quentin thrust his head forward and bit deep into Kaltenbrunner's skull, crushing his jaw, collapsing his temple, his other eye popping free, his teeth separating from the gums. Quentin twisted furiously until the flesh of Kaltenbrunner's neck split apart and his spine cracked- finally silencing his impetuous cries- allowing him to pull his head free from his body. Quentin held his trophy between his teeth for a moment, relishing its taste- the taste of victory, the taste of freedom, the taste, Quentin believed, of justice- before he began to eat.

Having escaped the Nazi's lair and discovered a payphone, Quentin pondered for a moment who he should call first—the police, a local television station; *Wave?* He settled on making an anonymous call to the authorities and informing them that a white supremacist terror cell had been responsible for the murder of a group of homeless men some many months before. No need to humiliate the poor souls still trapped in the zoo by parading them across the six o'clock news.

Quentin would learn only later of the subsequent

raid on the compound, spoken of in ellipticals by local news crews as a "domestic terror investigation;" stories spread via internet message boards of the people found inside, the victims of grotesque experimentation, who, it was said, were provided high-level care by prominent surgeons working under conditions of strict anonymity, and later given large sums of money in exchange for attesting any lingering signs of injury or mutilation to causes common and benign- car accidents; home-repair mishaps; drunken misadventure during the periods of dissolution and addiction that served as the convenient cover stories for their absences from polite society. As to the perpetrators of these abominations, the same message boards would speak- at once more accurately and more fantastically- of a Nazi eugenics program being operated, ostensibly, by everyone from the Illuminati to Lizard People to mole men to a cabal of wealthy, Los Angeles-based vampires. Quentin himself never prescribed much credence to any theory that called for a belief in the fantastical; despite what had become of him, his lived experience had taught him that man required no supernatural motivation for barbarity- merely the opportunity, the callousness, and, Quentin would argue, the dissatisfaction with one's own self to seek meaning in the suffering of others.

For a particular stripe of individual, Quentin had learned, cruelty was its own reward.

Those were all matters he would contemplate months, if not years, after his escape from the abattoir, however.

By the time police and FBI agents were investigating the scene, he had already set up shop in his warehouse, obtained through a quick series of phone calls to his attorney and a local real estate agent. Next had come the laptop order over the phone from a local electronics store and a series of impromptu conference calls with his old banks to assess the state of his financial affairs; and then had come the furniture, the wall art, the resettling into an old life- different now, in many respects, but in so many others like slipping his foot into a well-worn and much loved shoe gone neglected for too long. God, Quentin reasoned, had smiled on him after all: He had allowed him revenge, He had allowed him survival, He had allowed him escape; and now the wheels were set in place to have his glorious reunion with Wave.

One day...

<u>SEVENTEEN</u>

2002

Quentin Sergenov looks in the mirror and grins wide, adjusting his hat. Despite his dinosaurian anatomy, has never felt like more of a man. What else is a man, after all, he thinks as he squirts Drakkar Noir beneath his massive jaw, but someone who accomplishes his goals? Who faces tremendous odds, an entire world of jeering individuals standing in one's way, and says 'fuck you?' He is like a warrior of old; a brave and fierce Spartan, an insurmountable berserker, an unstoppable legionary.

Quentin saunters into his bedroom and looks at the two men who only moments ago regained consciousness. Their eyes gaze up at him in wide terror, their mouths sealed by duct tape, their wrists and ankles spread eagle and attached to either end of the bed with nylon rope tied into immaculate butterfly knots. The beauty of the tableaux is nearly paralyzing. Quentin's breath hitches in his chest and he lets out a long and plaintive sigh. There is only one thing missing. He moves to the record player and lets the needle drop. OMD's "Goddess of Love" fills the air and it's *perfect*.

"Hello Wave," Quentin says softly, as the music begins to play. Immediately both Wave and Griever register the voice, and each man begins to scream against their gags. Quentin moves to Wave and tousles the red wig secured to his head. "Shhh. I know. I was scared at first too. I've been through so much to get to here, Wave, so many terrifying and painful times and things. But it's OK now. I'm back. And now we can be together. We could never exist in *their* world...*that* world, that didn't understand us. But you see, I've created my own world now. In here. I've done it, you see? I've transcended everything: hated, bigotry, time, space... I've made this place, just for us. Just us. I've done it. *Ducky is going to win this time. You're* going to win."

Wave's eyes dart from Quentin to the *Pretty in Pink* wall mural. It occurs to him now, a logical thought penetrating the veil of terror in his mind, that Quentin is wearing a windowpane sportscoat, a porkpie hat perched atop his head and a Sony Walkman draped around his neck. Acknowledging this he turns to Griever and sees that his paramour is dressed in a twill blazer and oxford shirt; via process of elimination, Wave surmises that he himself has been dressed in a bright pink, custom-tailored prom dress.

"The story of our life," Quentin says, seeing that Wave has recognized the parallels between the mural and his present condition. "The studio made them change the ending, you know. The audience didn't like it. They *made* Andie reject Duckie. Just like the audience didn't like us. Just like Frank made you reject me. And I've watched it so many times, so many *many* times, trying to *make* it change. And then, one night, just the other night-- as a matter of fact, the night that I found out you were coming to town-- it *happened!* I was watching it...and *Andie chose Duckie!* After *all* this time, it just...*was* . And that's when I knew that it was time. Time to come get you. To show you the world I'd made. For me, and you...and him."

Quentin's eyes bulge from his sockets as they gaze at Griever. Griever whimpers through his gag and the last remaining drops of urine in his bladder soak through his white dungarees.

Quentin moves away from the bed and turns on the television set mounted to the wall. He grabs the skeleton in the rolling chair and pushes it aside so that Wave and Griever have a clear view of the screen.

"I made this for us," he whispers, a hint of pride in his voice.

The screen bursts to life. A jazz riff blares from the television's speakers. Split-second images of James Spader, a tyrannosaurus rex, Ensign Steele and Ensign DuFrense explode across the screen at breakneck pace. Quentin saunters back to the bed and mounts it, standing over Griever and Wave as the images onscreen reflect in their pupils. Griever begins to scream; Quentin grips his head in his claws and coos to him.

"Come and see," he whispers. "Come and see."

Quentin lies down on the bed between the men, looking back and forth between them, then to the screen, then back to Griever and Wave again, their faces turning away, their eyes shutting tight against the visual assault, and each time they look away or close their eyes Quentin playfully swipes at them with his tail and their gaze returns to the screen.

The film finishes; Quentin sighs. "Did you like it?" He addresses this question to Griever. "It was my parting gift to you."

Griever's eyes widen. He does not know how to take this statement.

"I want you to know," Quentin says, turning to Wave now, "That everything I have done, everyone I have destroyed, everything I have become, was because of love. Love of you. Some men say that they would walk through Hell, die, kill for those they love. Well I have done all of those things, Wave, for you. I've died. And I've killed. And I've walked through Hell. And I kept on walking straight back until I was with you again. Did I ever tell you that I was abused as a child, Wave? I'm not sure I did. Well I was. My stepfather, Mr. Tibbins? I mentioned him to you once or twice, I know that. I told you he was a sore subject. He used to beat me. After I came out to him. He told me that he was going to beat the sin out of me. And as he was doing it, he would tell me that I was unlovable. That he alone could care for me. That I should be forever in his debt that he had taken in this rotten little boy, clothed him, fed him, bathed him. He said that the world hated me. And I believed that for so long. I believed that I was the world's toilet- only good enough to be shit on and walked away from until someone needed to use me again to get rid of their own filth. And then there was you. And you loved me. And you held me. And you showed me that the world wasn't hate, like he made it out to be. That there was beauty in it, and that I could be a part of that beauty. And as you loved me, I loved you. I'd thought, for so long, that Mr. Tibbins had beaten the love right out of me. That I wasn't capable of it anymore. That I was going to end up some kind of monster. And then you showed me the light. And that's why I had to come back for you."

Quentin now turns to Griever.

"I finally came to understand, why he would pick you. Because you were just like us, after all, weren't you? An outcast. A reject. Tossed beneath the wheels of society because of who your heart told you to love. And then I didn't hate you anymore. I didn't want to destroy you anymore for replacing me. I understood that he wasn't rejecting me by loving you...He was only trying to fill the void that I'd left. And if there was a void left, that I meant something to him. You're an evidence of our love. You *are* our love. And you're going to stay here, with us. Forever."

Griever and Wave both begin to scream at the same time.

"Andie chooses Duckie this time, Blaine," Quentin says, gently, lovingly, as he opens wide and begins to devour Griever alive. He begins at the feet, the

Gucci loafers, the Calvin Klein underwear. When it is over, there is only a cleanly picked skeleton left strapped to the bed by frayed nylon ropes.

Wave stares up in horror as Quentin looms over him; he sees now not a grotesque caricature of Jon Cryer, but a giant, fanged raptor— a *mother* raptor—opening her beak to feed her young.

Quentin removes Wave's gagging just in time for his opened mouth to receive the regurgitated bits of Griever streaming out from between Quentin's teeth. Quentin rubs Wave's throat, firmly but with great care, ensuring that Griever goes down smoothly. The process takes several minutes; when it is finished Quentin feeds Wave a glass of water and re-gags him.

"He's with us now," Quentin says. "Our love. With us forever." He curls up beside the bawling Wave on the bed and kisses his face softly. "I know you're sad now. But we have all the time in the world for things to get better. Everything is going to be OK. We're together now. Forever. And ever. And ever and ever and *ever…*"

EIGHTEEN

Forever

Quentin Sergenov dozed off that night undisturbed in his sleep and content in his heart, and remained that way until the end of his days.

Acknowledgements

Any story is the product not only of the author but the people in their lives whose influence, feedback, encouragement, and insight are ultimately synthesized through the author's brain and end up in the finished narrative. So it is that I would like to thank the following individuals for their own contributions to bringing Quentin to life.

First and foremost, sincere gratitude (and my deepest apologies) to John Waters, whose films were a tremendous influence on me in college and integral not only to helping me develop my own narrative voice in general but specifically in realizing Quentin and his world.

Tremendous thanks go to B.J. Coleangelo, Jacob Larimore, and Robin-Anderson Forbes, who were kind enough to look at Quentin in some of his earlier incarnations and provide feedback that was invaluable in ensuring that the book did not harm, demean, misrepresent or otherwise negatively impact the LGBT+ community. It was imperative for me to have LGBT perspective on this story and they took their time not only to read the book but to point out aspects of the story that could be seen as offensive.

Thanks as always to my wife, Kayleigh, and my brother, Brian, my two oldest and most dedicated readers, who went on the entire, fifteen-year-long Quentin journey with me. I love you both.

A big shout out to Mark Miller, who's been a fan of my work since the beginning; without his patronage and his belief in this singularly insane story, you wouldn't be holding this book in your hands right now.

A final salute to The Nord, The Greatest Band in the World, gone but not forgotten. The Summer of 2003 will reign eternal in my memory. RIP

A general thanks, in no particular order, to the friends, supporters, allies, and confidantes who helped me through the evil Summer of 2020: Jessie Hobson, Barbara Crampton, Izzy Lee, Bradley Steele-Harding, Dan Gremminger, Jason Alvino, Katelyn Nelson, Chris Grosso, Matt Konopka, Grady Hendrix, Katie Rife, Ashley Laurence, Kelli Maroney, Phil Nobile Jr., k, Mitch McLeod, Jacob Knight, Jinx, Clay Neigher, Brandon Lyles, Tyler Liston, Ryan Larson, Max Booth III, Heidi Moore, Mike Vaughn, Chris Vander Kaay, Hunter Wayne, Adrienne Clark, Chris Panatier, Anya Stanley, Sadie Hartmann, Jon Abrams, Caroline Williams, Mike Vanderbilt, Danielle Ryan, John Fisher, Cory Brown, Mick Garris, Natasha Pascetta, Rachel Wilson, Josh Millican, Brandon Waites, "Mad" Ron Roccia, Lisa Hobbs, Brandon Wainerdi, Andrew Henderson, Leslie Hatton, Hector Rodriguez Gonzales III, Rebekah McKendry, and everyone else I'm probably forgetting. I can say with a lot of certainty that I may not be here without you and I'm eternally grateful for all you've put into my life.

About the Author

Preston Fassel is an award-winning writer whose work has appeared in *Fangoria, Rue Morgue, Screem*, and on *The Daily Grindhouse, Dread Central*, and *Cinedump. com*. He is the author of the first published biography of British horror actress Vanessa Howard, *Remembering Vanessa*, which appeared in the Spring 2014 issue of Screem. His debut novel, *Our Lady of the Inferno*, won the 2019 Independent Publisher's Gold Medal for Horror and was named one of the ten best books of the year by *Bloody Disgusting*.

www.ingramcontent.com/pod-product-compliance
Lightning Source LLC
Chambersburg PA
CBHW010348220726
48290CB00016B/2681